TIDES, TRAILS AND TROUBLE

DUNE HOUSE COZY MYSTERY

CINDY BELL

CONTENTS

*M*ary turned away from the kitchen sink as she heard footsteps behind her. She saw Suzie, carrying a few bags of groceries.

"Oh, Suzie you should have let me know, I would have helped you through the door."

"It's all right, I made it okay." Suzie smiled. "I checked the voicemail while I was out, and one of the guests requested a large birdcage." Suzie raised an eyebrow as she set down the bags of groceries on the counter. "Any idea where we can get one?"

"I already got one, actually." Mary smiled proudly. "I listened to the voicemail this morning while you were out, and I searched through some local sales pages and came across one for sale. It wasn't too much. Wes was coming over for a coffee

1

anyway, so he picked it up for me on his way here. I hope that's okay."

"Of course it is, you're a lifesaver. I wasn't looking forward to having a conversation with Mrs. Panner about why we couldn't get her a birdcage. The strange thing is, when I called her back, I asked her what kind of bird she would be bringing, and she said she wasn't bringing a bird. So, what could she possibly need the cage for?"

"I have no idea, but I'm looking forward to finding out." Mary laughed as she began to unload the groceries from the bags. Nothing made her more cheerful than new guests. In this case, they were part of a birdwatching group.

"Me too. Before I went to the store I stopped by the library and picked up all of the local bird information I could find. I think Louis thought I'd lost my mind." She pointed to one of the bags near the end of the counter. "They're in there. I also asked Jonathan to host a nature walk through the woods on the beach. They'll be by themselves for most of the birdwatching, but I thought with his local knowledge it might be a good way to introduce them to the area."

"Good idea, Suzie." Mary put the last of the groceries on the shelf, then turned back to face her.

"I'm sure they will all be thrilled. Was Jonathan any friendlier this time?"

"A bit." She grinned. "I managed to coax a smile out of him. I think he's just a little shy."

"That's possible. He's so young, he's probably still defining his role in life." Mary smiled to herself. "My son struggled at his age. Ben was so shy."

"I'm still trying to define mine." Suzie laughed. "If it weren't for inheriting this house and turning it into a bed and breakfast with you, I have no idea where I would be."

"It's changed my entire life, too, Suzie. We're very lucky."

"Yes, we are." She gave her friend a quick hug. "I'm going to check over the rooms one last time. Our guests should be arriving in the next hour or so."

"Let me know if there's anything you need help with. I'm just going to be putting together a welcome tray." Mary started towards the refrigerator. She usually put out a spread to welcome new guests. It was a warm way to greet them, and a great way to get to know them. People were much more talkative when there were snacks.

Suzie headed up the stairs to the guest rooms. On the second floor, she checked each room and

3

bathroom to be sure it had fresh linens and towels available. She knew everything would be fully stocked, but it was a routine she always went through before guests arrived. Even though there were no guests staying on the third floor, she checked that nothing was out of place. Guests often went up to the third floor to look at the view.

As Suzie walked down the hallway she paused to gaze out through one of her favorite windows in the house. It was in between rooms and larger than most of the others. It provided a view of the open expanse of beach beyond the back of the house. It still surprised her that she lived in such a paradise, all because of an uncle she barely knew.

A little further down the beach she could see the colorful tops of tents pitched by a group of surfers. That area of the beach allowed camping, and the group spent most of their time out on the water. She could see a few people in the distance riding the waves.

Even though Garber didn't attract many tourists, it was the type of place that people loved to visit, and she was lucky enough to live there. She tore her attention away from the beach and headed back downstairs to help Mary with last-minute things in the kitchen.

When she reached the bottom of the stairs a familiar nose nudged the palm of her hand. She drew back a bit at the wet touch, then laughed.

"Hello, Pilot." She rubbed her hand across the dog's golden fur. "How did you like your new bed, hmm?"

"He didn't use it." Mary smiled as she set a tray down on the butcher's block in the kitchen. It was filled with sliced vegetables, crackers, cheese, and assorted fruit. "He slept in my bed, again."

"Oh, Mary." She wagged her finger at her. "If you don't break him of that habit he'll never be out of your bed."

"I don't mind." She reached down and stroked the yellow Labrador's back. "When my kids were little they would pile into bed with me. It was the best feeling ever to be surrounded by love. Pilot keeps me warm, and you know, he's still grieving."

"That's true." Suzie studied the dog with a bit more empathy. He'd lost his owner recently, and had since barely left their side. If he wasn't with Mary, he was following Suzie around. Now and then he would chase the seagulls away from the property. Most of the time he was a very mild-mannered dog with a friendly lick for anyone that offered their hand. She'd double-checked with all of their guests to be sure the dog wouldn't be an issue, and all seemed quite enthusiastic to meet him. He'd become more than just a pet. He was a member of the family, and even of the town. Often people from the town would stop by just to pet or play with him.

"Did you check with Jason to make sure that he and Summer will be joining us for dinner?" Mary washed her hands in the sink then grabbed a towel to dry them.

"Yes, I texted him earlier. He said they'll be here unless disaster strikes. It must be tough that when there's a suspicious death they both get pulled into it. Jason investigates, and Summer examines the body. I wonder what they talk about at night." She raised an eyebrow. "Murders?"

"Or maybe anything but. I bet they need a break from the tension in their days. Maybe Jason rubs her feet." Mary grinned.

"Jason does what?" His familiar voice greeted them just before Pilot raced towards the door. Jason stepped inside with a grin.

"Some watchdog." Suzie rolled her eyes and laughed. She hugged her cousin. "How are you today, Jason?" In his thirties, it still felt as if he was young enough to be her son, and that sense of family pride welled up within her every time she saw him.

"Just checking on you two before the bird-watchers get here. I hope they're a tamer bunch than the surfers camped out on the beach. That group has been keeping me busy." He rubbed the back of his neck.

"I'm surprised you're not out there surfing with them." Mary eyed him. "You're too young to have body aches, you know? Too much stress isn't good for you."

"Thank you, Mary." He smiled at her with warmth in his eyes. "I prefer to surf without a crowd. But, you're right about the stress."

"What have they been up to?" Suzie glanced towards the window. "I haven't noticed much."

"It's mostly when they go into town. A few arguments here and there, usually between the members of the group. There are some heavy drinkers in the crowd. I thought surfers were supposed to be pretty laid back, but with this group it seems there's nothing but tension in it." He shook his head. "You would think the beautiful weather would chill them out."

"That does seem odd." Mary held out the tray to him. "Snack?"

"Those are for your guests." He waved his hand.

"And family. Go on, eat something, you're getting so thin."

"I am not!" He laughed as he plucked a piece of cheese. "I've put on at least fifteen pounds since Summer and I got married. She hasn't said anything, but I'm sure she's wondering if I'm pregnant." He patted his slightly rounded stomach.

"Oh please." Suzie rolled her eyes. "You're gorgeous and you know it." He was fit, tall, with a shock of red hair that drew the attention of all the ladies, especially his wife, Summer.

"Thanks." He winked at her. "I love stopping by here, I get licked, fed, and complimented."

"And you always will." Suzie smiled. At about twenty years his senior, she imagined he might see her as a mother figure, but it was Mary that did most of the mothering.

"I should get going, but I'll be back for dinner, and I promise to bring Summer. But I'm not rubbing anyone's feet." He gave them each a stern look, then turned and headed out the door.

Suzie and Mary laughed as the door closed behind him.

"No foot rubs?" Suzie frowned as she glanced over at her friend. "What's the point of getting married if no one rubs your feet?"

"Oh, he's rubbing her feet all right." Mary grinned. "What a good guy he is. She's lucky, but he's just as lucky, too."

"It's a beautiful match." Suzie nodded. "Speaking of matches, how are things going with Detective Wes?"

"Stop, you're going to make me blush." She laughed. "Oh look, they're here!" She pointed through the window by the front door as a car wound its way through the circular driveway. Pilot barely lifted his head as they walked towards the door. He was accustomed to guests and didn't bark when they arrived. However, once he was given the okay, he would accept petting from anyone that offered.

Suzie pulled open the door as a group of five people approached the front porch. Two cabs were parked in the driveway, and two drivers were unloading the trunks. The first person to mount the steps to the porch was a man who appeared to be in his sixties. He moved with a fluidity that surprised her, it reminded her of the grace a dancer would possess.

"Hello there, we're so glad we're finally here." His voice was just as smooth as his smile. "Bert Harrisons." He thrust his hand towards Suzie.

"Welcome." She smiled in return as she shook his hand. "I'm Suzie, and this is Mary, we run Dune House."

"It's a pleasure to meet you. Allow me to introduce the group." He gestured to the two couples behind him. "Callie and Herb Panner, as well as the youngsters over here, Tammy and Sebastian Northorn."

Callie and Herb held hands as they nodded to everyone. They appeared to be in their forties. Tammy and Sebastian looked to be closer to their early thirties.

"We're so glad that you are all here." Mary gestured for them to step through the door. "I have refreshments waiting and we'll get you all settled in."

"It was such a difficult flight." Callie frowned as she followed the group inside. "You'd think things would be smoother now than they were twenty years ago, but it seems that things only get more difficult. Do you know they made me take my shoes off in the security area? Have you ever heard of such a thing?"

"Forgive my wife." Herb narrowed his eyes. "It's been a long time since she's been on a plane."

"That's true. Only one thing could get me to

climb aboard one of those death traps. The possibility of sighting a Little Furn with my own eyes. It's the last domestic bird on my list. After this, we'll have to travel the world to see the rest, won't we, Herbie?"

"Yes, dear." He offered her a tight smile. "Which is why you're going to have to get used to being searched at the airport."

"I just think it goes a bit too far. I mean honestly, people need their personal space."

"Oh boy!" Suzie laughed. "Yes, it can be very unsettling."

"Why do you say such things, Callie?" Herb shook his head, his tone was sharp. "You embarrass yourself."

"I happen to agree with her." Mary grinned.

"I used to work as a personal bodyguard and when I went through training for my license we spoke to several police officers and guards in different positions. The stories they told about what they found hidden, is alarming to say the least." Sebastian plucked some cheese from the tray and popped it in his mouth.

"Okay, new topic." Bert clapped his hands. "How about this spread everyone?" He met Mary's eyes. "You are truly a wonderful host to know that we'd arrive hungry and tired."

"Travel can make anyone weary." She gazed at him. "Please help yourself, and if there's anything you need, all you have to do is ask. Suzie and I like to make sure our guests have the best experience here that they possibly can."

"Oh, I just can't wait to get out into those woods." Callie had drifted to the windows that over-looked the beach, and the woods in the distance. "This is such an amazing place. Look at how beautiful that water is."

"Not as beautiful as some of the beaches I've seen." Sebastian shrugged. "But it certainly is nice to look at."

"We can't all be international travelers like you and Tammy, Seb." Herb joined Callie near the window. "At least not until I can convince her to leave the States."

"Once she does, she'll never stop." Tammy smiled as she slipped an arm around her husband's waist. "When Sebastian and I decided to give up work, start our own business, and travel as much as possible, it was scary at first. But once we took off, we never wanted to land again. We are always waiting for our next adventure. Joining this birdwatching club is probably the tamest thing we've done in the past five years, but it's also been very rewarding. It's been a lot of fun to get to know all of you, and since this is the last bird on our list, I think this is the perfect place to celebrate our friendship and our accomplishment."

"I couldn't have said it better myself." Bert nodded as he filled a plate with food. "When I heard there was a possibility of seeing our last bird, the Little Furn, here, I knew we had to check it out. Plus, I've read great reviews of this place."

"I'm glad to hear that." Suzie walked over to join them. "A local guide, Jonathan Marows has offered to take you on a tour this afternoon if you're up for it. But we can always reschedule for tomorrow if you'd rather rest up a bit first."

"Absolutely not, we're ready to dive in, aren't we?" Callie clapped her hands with excitement. "Oh, did you get that birdcage?"

"Yes, I did, it's in your room. Would you like me to show you?" Mary gestured towards the stairs.

"That would be great, thanks."

"I'll bring up the bags." Suzie walked towards the luggage, but before she could pick up a bag Bert placed his hand on her shoulder and guided her away from them.

"I don't think so, not when I'm around. Sebastian, do you want to help me out here?" He gestured to the bags.

"Sure thing, Bert." Sebastian walked over.

"Really, it's fine." She smiled. "I do this all the time."

"That may be true, but on my watch, a lady does not carry luggage." Bert winked at her.

Suzie held her tongue. She had a lot to say about what she thought about that, but she knew that she had to be polite to her guests. As kind as the gesture was, she wasn't the type of woman to be told what she could or couldn't do, no matter the intentions. Instead she managed a soft nod.

"Thank you both. Mary will show you your rooms, and if there's anything that needs to be adjusted just let us know. Our goal is your comfort."

"Wonderful." He picked up a few of the bags and Sebastian grabbed the rest. Herb was engaged in a quiet, but tense conversation with Callie.

"I can't believe you asked them for a birdcage. I asked you to stop with that nonsense, didn't I?"

"There's nothing wrong with manifestation, Herb. If you tried it once in a while you might be a happier person."

"It's ridiculous is what it is." He rolled his eyes.

"If you don't like it, you don't have to look at it." She huffed, then stormed up the stairs after Mary. Herb stepped out the side door onto the porch and closed the door behind him.

Suzie glanced between the two, but did her best to pretend that she didn't hear their conversation. She couldn't help but wonder what the issue with the birdcage was.

"Excuse me, how early are we allowed down onto the beach?" Tammy collected some food on a plate as she spoke.

"There is no specific time, you're welcome to be on the beach whenever you'd like. There's no lifeguard, so you will be swimming at your own risk if you go into the water. Currently, there are some surfers camping on the beach, so you may run into them if you go out early."

"Oh no, I won't be in the water. My husband and I are martial artists, and we train early in the morning. I was hoping we'd be able to do so on the beach."

"Absolutely. We serve breakfast at eight, but the cabinets are always stocked with food, as is the fridge, so if you want to eat earlier you are welcome to help yourself." She studied the woman for a moment. She had shoulder length, dark wavy hair, and serious dark eyes. She was quite fit, and Suzie could sense that she had a certain level of confidence that probably came from life experiences. She was quite curious about what those experiences might be.

"Thanks, that's great." Tammy gazed out the window at the water.

CHAPTER 2

*A*s Mary led the rest of the group up the stairs, Herb's comment lingered in her mind. It wasn't just his words, but the way he spoke to his wife. Callie didn't seem to mind, but maybe that was worse. If she was so used to being spoken to that way, then how many years had it gone on for? She was startled when Callie stormed up the steps behind her. Maybe she minded more than Mary realized.

"Sebastian, I have you and Tammy set up in here." Mary pushed open the first door for Sebastian. "There should be plenty of closet space, but if you need any extra storage there are some closets in the hall for overflow. Also, I change the towels in the bathroom each morning, if you need more there should be plenty in the closet, but if not be sure to let me know."

"Thanks, I'm sure everything will be fine." Sebastian set down a few bags in the room. "Where is Callie's room?"

"Here." Mary gestured to the room beside Sebastian's. "We put everyone on the same floor. Bert, your room is at the end there beside the window."

"Thanks." He nodded to her then stepped into the room.

Sebastian set Callie and Herb's bags in their room, then smiled at Callie.

"Looks like you have a nice room here."

"Yes, it does," Callie agreed as she walked around the interior of the room and admired the decorations. "How beautiful."

"Suzie has experience as an interior decorator. She's created some amazing spaces for everyone to enjoy." Mary gazed with admiration at the décor. As much as she loved to cook and create she had never been great with design. However, Suzie could look at an empty space and envision something stunning. "I have some brochures, local maps, and restaurant suggestions downstairs if you'd like to take a look at them. Anything I can do to make your stay more enjoyable, just let me know."

After Mary had shown Sebastian and Tammy their room she headed back down the hallway. She paused at Callie's room.

"Will this be all right for you and Herb?"

Callie glanced over her shoulder and offered a mild nod, then she looked back at the birdcage that Mary set up near the window.

"This is perfect, thank you for getting it."

"Of course. Do you need any help with it?"

"No, I've got my precious settled in." She stepped aside to reveal a tiny bird perched on the swing in the middle of the birdcage.

"Oh, I didn't realize you were bringing a bird. I thought—" Mary cleared her throat as she realized that the bird was not a real bird, but a small stuffed bird.

"Yes, I know, it seems a little strange. I appreciate you indulging me. I believe that if I want something, I can manifest it. So, having a visual representation of a Little Furn helps me to manifest seeing it in real life. Of course, I don't want to actually keep one in a cage, well maybe I do, but I wouldn't." She smiled. "The bird is much too rare to keep as a pet. But this way I will always have one, and just maybe, I'll have the chance to see a real one." She looked over at Mary. "Nuts huh?"

"I don't think it's nuts at all." She smiled. "It's a great way to focus on your goal. If you need anything, be sure to let me know."

As Mary headed down the stairs she thought about the wistful tone in Callie's voice. She truly seemed to think that seeing this bird was going to be a miracle in itself. She hoped for her sake, she would get the chance to see one. But she also wondered what would happen after that. Would Callie have a new goal to set her sights on?

As she reached the bottom of the stairs she found Suzie cleaning up the snack tray from the table, and Tammy standing at the window that overlooked the beach.

"Did everyone get settled in okay?" Suzie led her into the kitchen.

"Yes, I think so." She frowned as she lowered her voice to be sure she wouldn't be overheard by Tammy. "I'm a little worried about Callie and Herb, though. Lots of tension there."

"Yes, but maybe it's just from all of the travel. It sounds like it was a bad day." Suzie began to wash the dishes in the sink. "You did a great job of welcoming everyone. Why don't you take Pilot for a stroll on the beach? He looks a little eager to get outside." She tilted her head towards the dog that stood near the back door.

"Ah, great idea. I could use a stroll." She smiled as she opened the door for Pilot. Although she had some pain in her knees, she always made an effort to walk. She hoped that eventually the exercise would strengthen them. Pilot ran right through the door and took off for the beach. Although he liked to run, he knew his limits. However, as he kicked up sand he didn't seem to notice the person sitting on one of the sand dunes.

"Hey! Watch it!" Herb jumped up and brushed sand off his shorts and shirt.

"Oh sorry." Mary called him over and kept him close as she didn't like the way that Herb looked at the dog. "He was just a bit eager to be outside. I didn't see you there."

"He should have better manners, or better yet you should put a leash on him." He sighed and brushed some more sand from his shirt.

"I'm very sorry, if it will make you more comfortable I will put his leash on, but he really is a very tame and friendly dog." She held up the leash she carried with her. "When I can, I like to let him have a little run."

"I understand. I'm the one that should apologize. The dog didn't do anything wrong. I'm just a little out of sorts today. Please, enjoy your walk." He sat back down in the sand.

"Travel can be so rough. I'm sorry you had a hard day, today." She stroked her hand through Pilot's fur. "Would you like to join us?"

"No thanks, when I'm like this, it's better if I'm left alone."

"I understand." She smiled at him once more, then led Pilot off down the beach. Pilot hung his head as he trotted along. "It's okay, boy, you're not in trouble. You can run!"

She laughed as the dog took off at a sprint. He skimmed the edge of the water with his paws, but didn't go too far in. Her attention shifted to the surfers in the water. They glided over the waves with such grace that it took her breath away. She could recall her son wanting to learn to surf. She'd taken him for lessons and after falling off dozens of times, he'd wanted to quit. She encouraged him to keep trying, and he did eventually get up on the board. But he lost interest fairly quickly. These men and women seemed to be very dedicated to what they were doing. Pilot jumped at the edge of the waves, then barked towards the surfers. She was a little surprised by that, and even more so when he began to bark wildly.

"Pilot!" She caught him by the collar and snapped his leash on. "I think it's time to get you home."

~

Suzie stepped through the back door and into the kitchen, then headed for the sink to wash her hands.

"I just finished weeding the back garden." She grinned at Mary as she put a platter in the refrigerator.

"Oh dear, you know Edgar will be upset that you touched his garden." She raised an eyebrow.

"I know." Suzie laughed. "That's why I did it. I still think it's funny when he gets so angry."

"Suzie! You shouldn't tease him so much. He's a great gardener." Mary couldn't help but laugh as well.

"Yes, he may be a great gardener, but he needs to lighten up a bit. Remember when I planted that tree and he insisted that it threw off the entire landscaping plan?" She shook her head. "I love his work, but it is still our property, isn't it?"

"Your property." Mary reminded her with a gentle nudge of her elbow.

"Ours." Suzie gave her a light hug. "I think I'll tag along with the birdwatching group, if you don't mind? I need a little more fresh air, this weather is too nice to ignore."

"Of course, go right ahead. I'm going to sit out on the deck and stare at the waves for a bit." She waved her hand in front of her face. "I got a little overheated in the kitchen."

"I bet." Suzie laughed and winked at her friend before she headed out the door to catch up with the birdwatching group. She met them at the edge of the woods. "Do you mind if I join you?"

"Hmm?" Bert looked over his shoulder. He eyed her for a moment, then nodded. "As long as you are quiet. We don't want anyone scaring away the birds. That guide you said would be here, hasn't shown up yet."

"I'll be quiet, promise. Oh, here he comes now." She smiled and waved to the man who approached. He was tall, thin, and in his twenties. With his shock of black hair, and sprinkle of freckles across his cheeks he stood out among the older crowd.

"Hello everyone. Sorry I'm a little late." He tipped his head back towards the campsite of the surfers. "I got caught up in a conversation with one of the surfers down there. A very wise, young man." He nodded to Suzie. "I'm so glad you're joining us."

After brief introductions, Jonathan led the way through the woods. As he walked, he shared some of the dangers of the woods, as well as unique flora that grew there.

"It's not often you find such a rich assortment of species, both plant and animal, in woods so close to the water. I consider these woods a rare and precious place. I ask that visitors treat them that way." He smiled as he looked over the group. "I am sure you are going to have some amazing experiences here."

"I'm sure we will," Bert murmured as he pointed towards a branch above Jonathan's head. "Look everyone, there's a Little Furn. I can't believe it, but all the markings are there."

A collection of whispered reactions rippled through the group. Suzie saw an adorable bird with a light blue body, splashes of pink on its tail feathers and head, and gray on its wings. She wasn't exactly sure why the others were reacting so strongly, but she was fascinated by it.

Callie clapped a hand over her mouth to muffle a gasp. She wiggled from one foot to the other, then fumbled for her camera which hung around her neck. Everyone in the group began to aim their cameras in the direction of the bird. Before anyone could snap a picture, a rustle of leaves and branches spooked the bird off its perch. The bird took flight and disappeared into the sky as a man stepped through the brush onto the path.

"You!" Bert exclaimed. "What are you doing traipsing through the woods? The path is clearly marked. There's no reason for you to be off it!"

"I'm sorry." The man raised his hands in the air as his eyes widened. "I was just doing some exploring. I wasn't aware that walking through the woods was an offense."

"It isn't legally." Jonathan frowned. "But it is discouraged. You're crushing flora, and entire habitats, if you stick to the path then you can enjoy the woods without causing destruction."

"Destruction?" The man chuckled. "It's the woods. Dogs poop in it. I think it'll survive."

"But will that Little Furn? You spooked it!" Sebastian seemed so upset that Suzie's heart began to beat faster. She sensed a conflict building. "We might never get to see it again. We might have missed our only chance. Little Furns are rare!"

"Oh no, oh no." Callie began to cry. She turned

towards Herb, but he shrugged her away. Tammy wrapped her arms around her instead.

"It's okay, Callie, I'm sure the bird will come back and we'll see it."

"I've done nothing wrong!" The man seethed in return. "I think you've lost your mind. The woods are the woods and I'll walk through them wherever I please."

"That's very disrespectful!" Sebastian lunged forward, but Bert stepped in front of him before the argument could come to blows.

"Sebastian!" Bert glared at him.

"Sebastian, calm down." Suzie frowned. "I'm sure that—" She paused and looked from Sebastian to the other man. "What is your name, sir?"

"Ken. Ken Barbar. I'm with the surfing group camping on the beach."

"See, Ken's from out of the area as well. He just didn't know. Did you, Ken?" She continued to look at him.

"Well no, but I still think it's kind of ridiculous. Everyone takes this love nature thing too seriously. I didn't mean to disrupt whatever you're doing here." He waved at the group. "I saw people, so I thought I'd come over and say hello."

"We were looking at a very rare bird." Bert

pointed down the path. "Maybe you're better off on the beach if you can't understand the value of a woodland area."

"And maybe you're better off not pointing fingers or trying to tell people what to do." His tall, muscular frame was a bit intimidating as he stood up straight and took a step towards Bert.

"Let's all just take a deep breath. All right?" Suzie looked between the three men. "There's no need for this to turn into anything ugly. The bird is certainly not going to return with all of this commotion. Let's just go our separate ways and forget all about this, all right?"

"Fine by me." Ken shrugged. "Good luck with your bird hunt, or whatever this is." He turned and headed down the path towards the beach.

"What a jerk." Sebastian huffed as he looked back at the others. "Honestly, someone should teach him a lesson."

"Listen, let's not let anything ruin our great moment. We saw a Little Furn, which means there may be more. Now you know where it was, you can come back here to watch for the birds. It's pretty exciting." Jonathan smiled. "Let's not lose sight of that."

"The bird probably won't come back." Callie's

chin trembled.

"Aw cut it out, it's just a bird." Herb threw his hands in the air. "We've seen it, now we can check it off on the list. Can we just move on, please?"

"Maybe we should break things off for today. I'm sure you'll have another chance to see the bird tomorrow." Suzie did her best to keep her tone soothing and calm. She could tell that the entire group was frayed at the edges and if the conversation was allowed to continue, more arguments would break out. "Remember, there is a beautiful beach out there to enjoy, plus lots of entertainment options in town."

"That sounds like a good idea." Bert nodded and patted Sebastian on the back. "Let's go blow off some steam, all right?"

"I guess." Sebastian tucked his phone back into his pocket. "Tomorrow is another day."

Suzie was relieved to head back to the house. She understood that the group was passionate about birds, but she never expected an argument to develop from it. When she reached the house, she found a note from Mary stating that she'd gone out for some last-minute groceries. She decided to immerse herself in a little reading to take her mind off the event in the woods.

CHAPTER 3

uzie woke up when her book fell out of her hand and struck the floor. She hadn't even realized that she'd fallen asleep. The scent of various spices filled the air as she took a deep breath. It drew her right down the stairs and into the kitchen. She loved it when Mary cooked. She cooked on occasion, too, but most of the time it was Mary that whipped up the evening meals. She had a special talent for creating delicious and interesting dishes. She never made the exact same thing twice, and yet the food was always amazing.

"Do you need any help with anything?"

"Just get the plates on the table, and we'll be ready to eat!" Mary smiled at her, a bit of sweat beaded across her forehead. "Stew, biscuits, and cheddar broccoli rice, what do you think? Too heavy?"

"Perfect!" Suzie's mouth watered as she gathered the plates from the shelf and carried them out into the dining room. The windows that lined the dining room overlooked the wraparound porch, and beyond it the beach. She could see Tammy and Sebastian outside on the beach, and Bert alone on the porch. He appeared to be watching them with great interest. She wondered for a moment about the solo man. He was quite handsome, and yet he traveled alone with two other couples. Was he just a loner by nature, by circumstances, or did he have a reason to avoid relationships? She finished putting the plates on the table just as Callie and Herb stepped in through the front door.

"Evening." Herb took off his hat and placed it on the hat rack beside the front door. Callie shrugged out of her light jacket and hung it on the hook under Herb's hat.

"Evening, you're just in time." Suzie smiled. "Doesn't it smell good in here?"

"Amazing!" Callie patted her stomach. "Which is great, because I'm starving. We've been wandering around town all afternoon, and I can't wait to eat!"

Suzie was relieved to see that she appeared to be in a much better mood than the last time she'd seen her. Herb was even smiling.

"It smells great." He nodded as he walked over to the dining room table.

A few minutes later, Jason and Summer arrived. Jason brought a bottle of local lemonade to share and Summer presented a side dish of her famous cinnamon sweet potatoes. Tammy and Sebastian joined Bert on the porch. Then all three stepped into the house. Once they were all settled at the table and introductions had been made, Bert pointed his fork at Jason.

"I'll tell you, there's one guy down at that camp on the beach that needs a stern talking to. His name is Ken Barbar. Can you speak to him and make sure he knows that he is to stay on the paths in the woods?"

"Well, I could speak to him." Jason dabbed his mouth with his napkin. "But it's not illegal to stray off the path. The best I can do is request that he be more cautious."

"That doesn't seem like enough." Bert sighed. "Sometimes I think the freedom in this country is a little out of control."

Jason looked down the table at Suzie, then glanced over at Bert. He started to open his mouth, but Suzie spoke up before he could.

"The important thing is that we can all share this beautiful place. I'm sure that Ken will be more careful now that he understands the damage he could do." She smiled sweetly at Bert.

Bert smiled in return, then focused his attention on his food.

Suzie and Mary exchanged a look at the end of the table. Mary knew there were times that they had difficult guests, but the birdwatching group seemed to be fixated on Ken. She only hoped that the animosity would fade overnight. Perhaps it was just the chaos of the day that had led Sebastian to be so upset. But she noticed that Callie's expression also shifted when Bert spoke of Ken.

"I'll tell you this much." Tammy looked over at her husband. "If I run into him again, and he is ignoring the safety and well-being of the creatures around him, Sebastian and I will both give him a reminder he won't easily forget."

"Listen." Jason set his fork down. "There is no reason to threaten anyone. I understand that you're all quite passionate about this, but please remember there is never a reason to resort to violence. If you run into an issue with Ken, just call me." He reached into his pocket and pulled out his wallet. Then he handed out his business card to each guest. "That's my cell number, any call will come to me directly, and I will be sure to respond quickly. All right?"

"Thanks." Bert nodded as he tucked the card into his wallet. "I will keep this handy."

The conversation shifted to what the group had experienced in town and things they might like to see during their visit. Suzie looked over at Jason with a smile of gratitude. He had defused what was becoming a very tense situation. It was quite a relief when everyone was settled in their rooms. It had been a strange day, and Suzie was glad to put an end to it. But as she lay in bed that night her thoughts turned to Paul, who was due to arrive home the next evening. No matter what stress might be occurring in her life the thought of seeing him always eased it for her. She was sure he would get a kick out of the stuffed bird in a cage. It would just be good to know that he was back on solid ground and available if she needed a break from the bird-watchers and the surfers.

*E*arly the next morning Suzie stepped into the kitchen and found no greeting from Pilot. Mary wasn't making breakfast yet, either, as it was only a little past six. Most of the guests were likely still sleeping. As she walked through the dining room she noticed Tammy and Sebastian out on the beach doing martial arts training. Their movements were timed together and fluid. She stepped outside to look for Pilot, as maybe he'd gone out when they did. However, after a quick search around the property she didn't find him, so she presumed he must be with Mary in her room. Maybe she was sleeping late.

As she stepped back in from the porch, Mary was there to greet her.

"Have you seen Pilot?" Mary asked.

"I was just looking for him. I couldn't see him anywhere. Usually he's here to greet me in the morning. I thought he was with you."

"I couldn't sleep, so we took a walk on the beach this morning. Just for a few minutes. I saw him run back to the house. But now I can't find him." Mary glanced around, then frowned. "Pilot!" She slapped her hands against her knees. "Here boy!"

They both listened for any sign of the dog, but the house remained silent.

"Where is he?" Mary walked towards the front door. "I'm going to go out and look for him. Something doesn't feel right."

"Wait, I'll come with you." Suzie followed Mary out the front door. As soon as they were outside they both began to call for Pilot. "Do you think he would head towards town?" Suzie looked in the direction of the road that led into town.

"Maybe. But my best guess, as friendly as he is, he probably went down to the surfers. I bet that's where he is."

"All right, let's take a look." Suzie fell into step beside her. They headed down the beach in the direction of the campers.

The first thing Suzie noticed was the lack of litter around the tents and campfire. She expected them to leave behind a lot of wrappers, cans, and other garbage. Instead it appeared that they did a good job of keeping their campsite tidy. Most of the surfers were out on the water, but a few were gathered around a small sand pit filled with an assortment of shells.

"My girlfriend back home makes jewelry out of

things like this." One of the men picked up a shell and held it up to the sunlight. "She's going to love this."

"Excuse me, have any of you seen a dog alone on the beach?" Suzie peered between the three faces. Two appeared to be in their thirties, while the third might not have even been twenty.

"Did you lose your dog?" The youngest man asked. "I'm Kai, this is Joel and Art." He tipped his head towards the two other men. Art set the shell back in the pit.

"Usually he doesn't wander far. We live up there, at the bed and breakfast." She gestured to the house. "I guess he might have found something to chase." She showed him a picture of the dog on her phone.

"Oh yes, I did see him. Just a little while ago. He was headed towards the woods. I can show you where, if you like." Kai smiled.

"Sure, that would be great." Suzie felt some relief, but she was still nervous. Why would Pilot be wandering in the woods? It was odd behavior for him.

Kai led them both to the woods, then down a thin trail. It wasn't one that Suzie usually walked.

"I took a walk with my dad this morning, and we saw him head this way. We called to him, but he didn't seem interested. We figured he knew his way home." He paused and peered through some branches. "Is that him?" He pointed to a fluff of yellow ahead of them.

"Yes!" Mary gasped. "Pilot, what are you doing?" She clapped her hands together. Pilot gave one last bark at a tree, then bolted back towards them. He didn't care that he trampled brush and broke thin branches as he ran past. Mary caught him by the collar and held on tight. "What were you chasing, you naughty boy?" She peered up into the tree and saw a squirrel a few branches up. "Ah, I see." She laughed.

"Thanks so much for helping us find him, Kai. We could have been looking for a long time." Suzie smiled.

"No problem. If I see him around here again I'll be sure to send him home."

"Thanks again." Mary led Pilot past him and back down the trail. "I think we'll have to keep him on the leash more often if he's going to start chasing squirrels."

"He doesn't usually do that." Suzie frowned as

they walked back towards the house. "I've seen him bark at a few and play a bit in the yard, but I've never seen him chase one. Do you really think he followed one all the way to the woods?"

"It's possible, he is a dog. But you're right, he doesn't usually chase things. We'll have to be more careful."

Pilot didn't seem to be bothered by his excursion. Instead he pranced right up onto the deck and began to sniff the boards for evidence of food.

Suzie shooed him into the house. "No more escaping for you. The last thing we need is for you to run into Ken Barbar, or do something to upset the guests."

"I should get breakfast going. I'm making cranberry orange muffins." Mary walked over to the sink to wash her hands.

"Oh, that sounds delicious, as always."

"Thank you. I'm glad we met that young man, Kai wasn't it? He was very nice." She turned on the oven to preheat then gazed out the window in the camp's direction.

"Yes, he was nice." Suzie washed up as well and pulled out some of the supplies that Mary would need to make the muffins.

"We should take some muffins down to them." Mary wiped her hands on a dishtowel, then turned away from the window. "I'm sure they can't be eating very well."

"I don't know, Mary, from what Jason said they can be a rough bunch. Are you sure we should get in the middle of that?"

"They can't be that bad. Last night they had a drumming circle. It was nice to hear the music from down there. There might be a few bad apples, but I bet there are some interesting people, too. Besides, Kai brought us to Pilot, right?"

"That's true. But if you're going to take a basket of muffins down there I'm going with you."

"Fair enough." Mary smiled.

Soon they were swept up in the rush of breakfast. By the time everyone had eaten and headed out the door, Mary was ready to make a break for it. She packed up a basket of muffins and looked over at Suzie.

"Ready for a walk?"

"Sure, let's keep Pilot on the leash this time." She called the dog over, gave him a good pat, then hooked his leash on to his collar. As they headed out the door, Suzie noticed that none of their guests were on the beach. Bert had mentioned something at breakfast about going on a birdwatching excursion first thing. She just hoped that Ken wouldn't be involved in that. As they approached the campsite, angry voices drifted towards them.

"Oh dear." Mary frowned. "I wonder if it's Sebastian and Ken."

"It doesn't sound like Sebastian." Suzie edged closer to the group.

"You said drinks and meals were included in this trip, Noel!" Ken shouted at a taller, thinner man. "It was supposed to be included in the total price, that's why I booked this trip!"

"You must have misunderstood, drinks and meals have always been extra, it's not like I have a fully stocked kitchen at the campsite." The tall man sighed.

"We haven't even managed to get a good day of surfing in." Ken scowled.

"I told you to surf early when the tide is high, but you didn't listen to me."

"What, do you expect me to get up at the crack of dawn?" He stared at him.

"You have to get up early so you can get the most out of the surfing here. I don't control the tides." The tall man raised his voice. "You've been nothing but trouble on this trip, I'll gladly refund your money, so I can be rid of you!"

"You'd like that wouldn't you, huh?" Ken shoved the man's shoulders. "I'm not going anywhere. My son and I are on this trip, and we're going to enjoy it the best we can. But you will be giving me my money back, and you'll be lucky if I don't sue you for false advertisement!"

"Dad, calm down." Kai stepped forward and placed his hand on his father's arm. "It's not that big of a deal."

"It is to me!" Ken shoved his son's hand away. "I know you're used to having money, but just because we're wealthy that doesn't mean that every penny doesn't count. It's ridiculous that you would run this con game and expect to get away with it. The advertisement clearly stated that drinks and meals would be included. That is what I paid for!"

"Again, you must be mistaken, that is not something that has ever been offered. You should really listen to your son." He shook his head, then turned and walked off across the sand.

"Is everything okay here?" Suzie gazed at Ken, then shifted her attention to Kai. She never would have pegged them for father and son, but now that she saw them standing beside each other she could see the resemblance.

"It would be better if I didn't book a vacation with a crook." Ken kicked some sand up into the air.

"Dad, please." Kai rolled his eyes. "This was supposed to be a vacation for us, so just let it be."

"I'm trying, Kai." Ken shoved his hands into the pockets of his shorts and gritted his teeth. "I'm trying."

"Maybe this will help." Mary held up the basket of muffins. "Something to sustain you while you're roughing it out here."

"Thanks." Kai smiled as he took the basket. "These are great. Right, Dad?"

"Actually, yes, I'm starving." He grabbed one of the muffins. "Thanks." He took a large bite as he walked off.

"Sorry about my dad, he has quite a temper. Thanks for the muffins." Kai carried the basket off to the others gathered around the campsite.

"Quite a temper doesn't exactly describe it." Mary frowned. "Ken is like a time bomb, waiting to explode."

"He does seem like a loose cannon. Hopefully he'll find a way to calm down. For Kai's sake, at least." Suzie turned and started back towards the house. "Let's do our best to stay out of it, all right?"

"All right." Mary nodded, but cast a glance over her shoulder in Kai's direction. Against the back-drop of the ocean he looked as young and innocent as her own son once had.

CHAPTER 4

*A*fter a busy day of cleaning the guest rooms, handling the laundry, and entertaining the guests, Suzie was relieved to put the dinner dishes in the sink.

Mary leaned heavily on the counter. "Wow, what a day, huh?"

"Yes, is it just me or did it seem especially draining?" Suzie shook her head. "Usually I'm excited about having guests, but all of the tension is just wearing on me."

"I know what you mean. I've been nervous about Ken all day. I hope he hasn't caused any more disruption. Bert said they didn't spot the Little Furn on their walk this morning, but he didn't mention running into Ken at all."

"That's a relief. Hopefully, we can get through

the next few days without them running into each other. As for Ken and the man he fought with on the beach this morning, that might just boil over into something that Jason will have to handle."

"Let's try not to think about it. Maybe tomorrow will be better. Doesn't Paul get in tonight?"

"Yes, I can't wait to see him. And you're right, I should put it out of my mind. I'm just going to take a cup of tea out onto the porch and relax a bit before he arrives."

"That sounds like a great idea. I think I'm going to turn in early and catch up on some reading. A good relaxing night should help restore my energy for tomorrow."

"Why don't you head to bed now? I can take care of these dishes. I'm going to be up anyway."

"Are you sure?"

"Of course." Suzie gave her a light hug. "Go, get some rest, tomorrow will definitely be better."

"Thanks, Suzie. Tell Paul I say hi."

"I will." Suzie turned back to the sink to wash the dishes. After she finished, she made herself a cup of tea, then headed out onto the porch. As she sipped her tea she gazed out over the water. The mid-light of dusk made her eyes strain just enough to create some tension in her head, but as she willed herself to relax, the pain eased. Finally, she saw what she was watching for, Paul's boat against the horizon. He would be docked soon, and would likely stop by to see her. Often, she would meet him at the dock, but with new guests in the house, she preferred to be present in case any issues arose. However, her heart was still at the dock, waiting for him. As impossible as it seemed to her that she had stumbled her way into romance, there was no longer a question in her mind that Paul was the man she'd been waiting to meet all of her life. She still valued her independence and it made her a bit concerned to think she was so vulnerable, but it was worth it, when she felt his arms around her. After over fifty years of believing that true love wasn't a real thing, Paul had proven her wrong.

As more time passed, she left her cup of tea on the table, and walked down towards the beach. She was sure that he would arrive fairly soon, and he would know to look for her on the beach. Her legs were itching to move, and the night sky drew her closer to the water's edge.

The moonlight pooled across the glassy surface of the ocean. It resembled a path, as if she could walk it, and discover something magical. When the wind blew, the water rippled and the path disappeared.

"There you are."

His familiar voice caused her to turn with a smile to face him.

"Just waiting for you, Paul." She drank in the sight of him.

"I'm sorry about that." He wrapped his arms around her waist. "I got caught up with some issues at the dock. I hit some rough seas on the second day, and I guess it did a bit more damage than I realized."

"Oh, I don't like hearing that." She rubbed her hands along his shoulders. "The thought of you in any kind of danger worries me."

"Well, don't worry." He smiled. "I was never actually in any kind of danger. But, the boat will need some repairs before I take it out again. Which means I get to spend more time with you. That can't be so bad, can it?"

"Definitely not." She kissed his cheek. "We have a few guests though, I'm going to be pretty busy."

"Anything I can do to help, just let me know."

"Thanks, Paul. I appreciate that. Just this is more than enough." She rested her head against his chest and breathed in the scent of his skin. He smelled like the ocean, mingled with the splash of cologne he always put on right before he saw her.

"How are the new guests?"

"Interesting, to say the least." She grinned. "But, it's always fun to have new people to get to know. I'm not so sure that they're going to get along with the surfers on the beach, though."

"No?" He leaned back and looked into her eyes. "What happened?"

"The birdwatching group and one of the surfers got into a bit of a skirmish over where he should be walking. It was all a bit silly to me, but those bird-watchers are passionate about their birds. I guess I can understand why they would be upset if he was disrupting the birds they came to see." She continued to fill him in on the run-ins with Ken and the tension between Callie and Herb.

"Another adventurous day in Dune House, hmm?" He kissed her forehead. "You are so much better with people than I am. I would much rather just spend my time with you."

"I like that about you." She laughed. "Now, do you really want to go for a walk or are you too tired? We can always just go sit on the deck and have some tea."

"I would never turn down a walk under the stars

with you." He pulled away and slipped his arm around hers. "Shall we?"

"Yes, we shall." She winked at him, then began to walk along the beach towards the woods. It was the best way to avoid the campers on the beach. She had no interest in running into Ken. "Isn't it gorgeous out tonight?" She sighed with pleasure as she soaked up the warmth of his hand around hers and the magic of the woods.

"It's perfect." He nodded. "As much as I love being out on the water, there's something beautiful about being surrounded by the woods as well. I just enjoy being immersed in nature."

"I agree. It changes my perspective entirely." She closed her eyes and took a deep breath of the night air. She opened them again when her foot struck something strange. She thought at first it was a root or a large stick, but the give in it made her realize it wasn't perfectly solid. Her stomach twisted, even before her eyes found the object she'd struck.

"Paul," she gasped out his name and clung to his arm to steady herself.

"What is it, sweetheart? You look so pale." His eyebrows knitted with concern.

"Paul." She couldn't bring herself to say

anything else as her eyes traveled up from the sandal on the foot to the board shorts, to the t-shirt, and finally to the face of the body that lay stretched into the woods.

"Oh my!" Paul finally looked in the same direction she was. "Stay back, Suzie!" He gave her a gentle shove out of the way then crouched down beside the body to check for a pulse. "He's not breathing, I'm going to start CPR!"

"Okay, I'll call for help and then I'll help you," she said, but she could tell it was too late. She fumbled in her pocket for her phone to call the ambulance and then Jason.

Shortly after hanging up from Jason she heard sirens.

"We're here," Suzie called out as she heard footsteps getting closer.

She sighed with relief when she saw the EMTs. They immediately moved Paul and Suzie out of the way and took over.

Paul held Suzie's hand tightly as they watched on.

"Who is it? Do you know?" Paul looked at her, shocked. She realized that she probably looked just as shocked.

CINDY BELL

"It's Ken Barbar. He's with the group of surfers that are camping on the beach. Or at least, he was."

"He's gone." The EMT shook his head as he looked at his partner. "Looks like a broken neck."

Suzie gasped at his words.

"Poor guy must have been up in that tree," Paul whispered as he pointed to a tall tree not far from Ken's body. Below a bird's nest high up in the tree, a few of the branches were broken off and some had just snapped and dangled from the thick trunk. "A fall from there couldn't have broken his neck, unless he landed on his head. Do you think he was drunk? Maybe he fell asleep and fell out of the tree?"

"I have no idea what to think." Suzie turned her head as she heard more sirens approaching.

Paul held Suzie close as a stiff breeze carried through the woods. The night which seemed so beautiful just moments before, now felt eerie. A pang of guilt carried through her as she recalled how happy she'd been.

"Suzie?" She heard rushed footsteps on the path from the beach. "Suzie, where are you?"

"Over here, Jason!" She pulled away from Paul and ran towards the sound of Jason's voice. As soon as he came into view, words began to spill out of her mouth. "Jason, it's awful. It's Ken Barbar, he's here

54

with the surf group that's been camping on the beach. Paul and I just went for a walk, and we found him." She shivered. "I think he must have fallen somehow."

"Fallen?" He followed her down the trail, then paused when he saw the body. "What makes you think he fell?"

"Broken branches." Paul pointed up at the tree. "I have no idea what he could have been doing up there, though."

"I'll take over things from here." Jason pulled out his radio and barked a few orders, then walked over to the EMTs. After speaking to them he turned towards Suzie. "Are you okay?"

"I'm okay." She nodded. "But the poor surf group, and his son. His son is here on the trip with him, he might be nineteen or twenty. Oh, this is so awful." She closed her eyes.

"We're going to go back to the house, Jason," Paul said.

"Good idea." Jason nodded as he waved a few police officers towards them. "I'll touch base with you as soon as we are done here."

Still dazed, Suzie and Paul walked back along the beach towards the house. The sirens had been cut off, but the garish blue and red flashes across the sand created a strange glow. She could see that the people on the beach had begun to mill around, curious about what was happening in the woods. Her stomach twisted as she thought of the moment when they would find out that one of their own had died. Kai would soon discover that his father was gone. As the thought rushed through her mind, she saw Mary ahead of her. She took the last step down from the porch, then ran towards Suzie.

"Suzie, is everything okay? I heard all of the sirens and then I saw the police cars." She pressed her hand against her chest. "I was so worried that something had happened to you or Paul."

"I'm sorry, Mary, I didn't even think of that, I should have called you." She pulled away from Paul, then embraced her friend. "I'm afraid something terrible did happen, but not to me or Paul. When we went for our walk through the woods, we came across Ken Barbar, he had a horrible accident, Mary, and he's gone."

"Gone?" Her eyes widened. "You mean he's dead?"

"Yes, I'm afraid so." Suzie shook her head. "Somehow he broke his neck. We think maybe he fell out of one of the trees and landed the wrong way."

"Fell out of a tree?" Mary took a step back and stared at her. "Are you serious about that?"

"Yes, I know, it doesn't make much sense. I'm sure Jason and Summer will figure out exactly what happened, but it may take some time. Did any of the guests wake up with all of the commotion?" Suzie asked.

"Not that I've seen. If they have, they haven't come down to talk about it. We should tell them though, before they find out through gossip." Mary gazed down at the beach and the path that led into the woods. "This is just awful. I'm not sure how we will be able to explain it. And, oh no!" She clasped her hand over her mouth. "Ken's son! Has anyone told him?"

"I assumed that Jason would tell him." Suzie rested her hands on the railing of the porch as she peered down at the campsite on the beach. "I don't see too much movement down there right now."

"I should go with him." Mary frowned. "A boy his age shouldn't be alone when he is told something like this."

"Do you want me to come with you?" Suzie met her eyes and slipped her hand around hers.

"No, you should stay here in case any of the guests figure out what's happening. I'll be okay. Let me just go put something more decent on." She tightened her robe, then stepped back into the house.

"She's such a kind woman." Paul rubbed his hand along Suzie's back. "She's right, he shouldn't be alone."

"I don't think I could face him right now. Mary's much better at that sort of stuff, anyway."

"You are pretty good at it yourself, but I'm sure she can handle it. You're going to come inside, and sit down, and let me make you a nice warm cup of tea." He raised a finger when she opened her mouth. "No arguing." His bushy eyebrows furrowed.

"Okay, no arguing." She sighed. She knew that look. Usually it made her want to argue more, but tonight, she was grateful for his insistence. She didn't think her legs could carry her much farther. After she settled on the couch, she closed her eyes. "What in the world would he have been doing in a tree?" She shivered. "It's not like there are any bears in the woods."

"Who knows." Paul called from the kitchen. "Maybe he was so out of it that he imagined something was chasing him."

"Or maybe someone?" She paused as Mary

came back down the stairs, followed by all of the guests.

"What's going on?" Bert stared through the front windows as the blue and red light reflected off them. "Did something happen?"

"Mary, you go on to Kai, I'll tell everyone." Suzie stood up. "Paul, I think we're going to need more tea."

"Coming up!" He nodded to Mary as she headed for the side door. "Are you sure you'll be all right on your own?"

"Yes, I'll be fine. Thank you."

As the guests gathered around the living room, Suzie realized she had quite a task ahead of her.

"I'm afraid I have some difficult news to share with all of you. I'm sure you all recall meeting Ken Barbar?" She looked between their faces.

"What has he done?" Bert scrunched up his nose. "Is it a fire? I was worried that campfire would spread to the woods, I bet they let it get out of control."

"He hasn't done anything, Bert." Suzie's tone was a bit sterner than she intended, but she was still shaken by the memory of finding Ken. "Unfortunately, he's had a terrible accident. He didn't survive it."

"He's dead?" Callie's voice trembled. She grabbed Herb's hand and held it tightly.

"What kind of accident?" Sebastian stood up from the couch, while keeping one hand on Tammy's shoulder. "Is it dangerous here? Was he out in the water?"

Suzie braced herself for even more questions. She knew that she wouldn't have the explanations that they were looking for, but she would have to try her best to provide them.

"He was in the woods. Somehow he fell. That's all we know." She frowned. "I know it's shocking."

Paul walked into the living room with a tray of tea cups and set it on the coffee table.

"How awful." Tammy shook her head. "What could he fall from in the woods? I don't understand."

"I don't quite understand, either. But Jason will find out exactly what happened, I can promise you that. I want you all to know that the woods are very safe. I'm sure that what happened to Ken was a freak accident, and not something that any of you should be worried about," Suzie said.

"That's easy for you to say." Herb hit his palm with his fist. "You know what happened. You're not giving us all of the details."

"I am, I don't know anything else. Let me get us all something to eat. I'm sure that Jason will stop by to fill us in when he has figured things out." She started to stand up, but Paul guided her back down onto the couch.

"No, you sit. I'll find something." He headed back into the kitchen.

Suzie sank back down into the cushions and did her best to field the questions that continued to come at her.

CHAPTER 5

A sense of dread filled Mary as she approached the trail that was now illuminated by floodlights. She could see that there were several officers around the area. She assumed that Kai might have already been informed. He might not want anything to do with her, but she would at least be available in case he did need someone to talk to. However, as she drew close enough to hear voices she noticed a tension between Jason and Kirk, his partner.

"I guess you know best then, I shouldn't have opened my mouth." Kirk took a step back just as Mary walked up.

"Jason?" Mary peered between the two officers. Kirk's cheeks were so red that she was sure he was either embarrassed or furious. "What's going on?"

"Mary, what are you doing out here?" Jason frowned as he turned away from Kirk.

"I was hoping I might be able to go with you when you talk to Ken's son. He's just a boy, and I thought maybe I could help to comfort him when you break the news." She lowered her eyes as Jason's expression was rather stern. "I'm sorry, I didn't mean to interrupt. I'm sure you've already told him."

"Don't be sorry. That's very considerate of you, and yes I would like it if you joined me. I haven't told him yet. Just give me one second and we'll head down."

"Okay." Mary's eyes lingered on the tarp that had been placed over the body. It felt strange knowing that Ken's body was there.

"All I'm saying is that you need to consider that it might not have been an accident." Kirk shoved his hands into his pockets. "Look, I'm the rookie here, I get it. But it doesn't make sense, does it? A guy like that climbing trees and falling out? He's an athlete."

"Just because he surfed, that doesn't make him an athlete. We don't know how fit and agile he was. We do know that the guys down there have been getting into trouble ever since they showed, for drinking and partying. So, our guy gets drunk, decides to pretend he's a monkey, and passes out. It's that simple. You can't look for a crime in every death, most deaths occur due to accidents or natural causes. In this case it looks like an accident."

"So, you won't even consider that someone might have done this to him?" He stared hard at Jason.

"I'll consider whatever the medical examiner tells me to consider. Until then, this is an accident. We'll keep the scene roped off until Dr. Rose declares an official cause of death. My focus right now, is to inform his son that he's lost his father, before someone else tells him. All right?"

"All right." Kirk nodded. He glanced at Mary, offered her a sad smile, then turned back to the other officers.

Mary fell into step beside Jason as he headed back down the trail towards the beach. Her heart ached for him. She was sure that having to make these kinds of notifications was not easy for him. He'd lost his own father not that long ago, and though they were never close, she was sure that the wound was still fresh in his mind.

"Thanks for coming with me, Mary." He tilted his head in the direction of the campsite. "I have a feeling this is not going to go well."

"I doubt it will." She frowned.

When they neared the campsite the light of the campfire flickered across the tents that were pitched in a messy circle around it. One man sat in the sand, not far from it. It only took her a second to realize it was Kai.

"Kai?" Her voice was soft as she tried to draw his attention.

Jason straightened up as he prepared to deliver the news.

"Mary." Kai smiled and stood up to greet her. "It's a beautiful night, isn't it?" His eyes shifted to Jason, who wore his uniform. "Were we making too much noise? Just about everyone is asleep."

"No, you weren't." Jason cleared his throat. "I'm afraid I have some difficult news, Kai. Your father is Ken Barbar?"

"Yes." Kai's eyes widened. The reflection of the flames across his tanned skin gave him an eerie glow. "What's happened? Is he all right? I told him not to go off so late."

"He's suffered a terrible accident, Kai. I'm sorry to tell you, he's deceased."

"Deceased?" He stared at Jason. "Is this some kind of joke?"

"No, Kai, it's not." Mary placed her hand on his

shoulder. "I know this is quite a shock, but your father has passed away. I'm very sorry for your loss."

"My loss." His shoulder tensed under her touch. "There must be some kind of mistake. What accident? How did this happen?"

"At this time, we believe that your father may have fallen from a tree and landed in a manner that took his life. His body will be taken to the medical examiner's office to confirm the cause of death. Can you tell me the last time you saw him?" Jason pulled out his notepad.

"This is unreal." He stumbled back a few steps. Mary slid her arm around his back to support him.

"It's a lot to take in, I know. Do you want to sit down?" Her voice was full of warmth.

"No, I'm okay." He shrugged off her touch and narrowed his eyes. "Are you sure this isn't some kind of mistake? It's definitely him?"

"He was identified by someone, and his wallet was in his pocket with his driver's license in it. However, you'll have the opportunity to identify him yourself. I understand how shocked you must be, but I do want you to know that we are doing everything we can to ensure that your father is treated with respect, and that his death is fully understood." Jason looked into the younger man's eyes. "Is there someone we can call? Your mother? Another relative?"

"No, don't." He hung his head. "She doesn't even know I'm here. She'll be upset when she finds out."

"Why would she be upset?" Mary studied him.

"My dad left her two years ago. Well, he cheated on her first, and then she caught him, and he left. She's furious with him, and so was I, I still am I guess. If she knew I came on a trip with him she'd be hurt."

"I see." Jason nodded. "So why did you come on the trip with him?"

"He offered to pay for me. I thought maybe we'd have a chance to talk things out." He lowered his eyes. "I know what he did was wrong, but you know, he wasn't the worst father." His voice cracked as his shoulders slumped. "I can't believe this. I can't believe that he's gone."

"I know it is a lot." Jason rested his hand on Kai's shoulder. "This is the last thing you could have expected. But I do need to get as much information as I can from you."

"I'll answer any questions you have, but I'm not sure how much I can tell you. All I know is that he got into another argument with the organizer of the trip, and he stormed off into the woods."

"This organizer, can you give me his information?" Jason jotted down the details that Kai gave him. "Thank you, Kai. Again, I'm very sorry for your loss. I'll be in touch with you about any changes in our investigation, and as soon as your father has been examined, the medical examiner will help you make arrangements. Are you sure you don't want me to call anyone for you?"

"No, thank you. No." He stared down at his hands, clearly dazed.

Mary stroked his back and frowned as she looked over his head at Jason.

Jason walked over to the rest of the group, while she remained with Kai.

"Sweetheart, I know you think your mother will be angry, but I can tell you as a mother, if my son didn't call me in this situation, I'd be quite upset. I think you should call. I can call for you if you'd like."

"You're right." He nodded as he wiped his eyes. "No, it's okay, I'll call her. Thanks, Mary, but I need to be alone while I do this."

"I understand. You know where I'll be if you

need anything. If you want to stay up at the house you are welcome to."

"Thanks." He nodded again, then stood up and walked towards the water.

Mary lingered for a few more moments to be sure that all was as well as it could be at the campsite, then headed back up to the house.

$\sim$

Suzie had just washed the last tea cup when Mary stepped back inside the house. She looked towards her as her heart sank.

"How did Kai take it?" She walked over to Mary and hugged her.

"He's in shock, I think. I convinced him to call his mother, but it wasn't easy." She filled Suzie in on the history between Kai and his father.

"So, this trip was a chance for them to reconnect. That makes things even worse. Ken might have been a man with a temper, but he certainly didn't deserve to die. Here, I'll make you some tea." She reached towards the cup.

"Thanks, Suzie, but I think I just want to go to bed. It's been quite a day. I told Kai if he needed some privacy and a place to sleep he could come up to the house. I hope that's okay."

"Of course, it is. Get some rest, Mary."

"Thanks." Mary trudged towards her room with the weight of the evening on her shoulders. It was hard not to think how she might feel if it was her own son enduring the loss of his father. Although there were some good times, her husband had been terrible to her, and when their marriage finally ended, it was very scary. She was sure that if it weren't for Suzie she would have still been adrift and trying to figure out what direction to take. Despite all of the history between herself and her husband she would never want her children to face the grief of losing him. Now Kai faced that, and she hoped that his mother would understand and be as supportive as he would need her to be.

Suzie carried the tea cup back into the living room, where Paul had fallen asleep on the couch. After his long journey on the water she knew he needed his rest. She on the other hand couldn't even think of closing her eyes. Her nerves were still frazzled and her mind churned with theories of what happened to Ken. No matter how she played out the event in her mind, she couldn't come up with a series of events that led to him falling out of a tree, or even climbing a tree in the first place. She wanted more than anything to believe that it was an accident, but she just couldn't figure out how it happened.

A few hours later, when she finally did close her eyes, her body ached with fatigue, and her mind still spun, unable to settle without a final verdict on Ken's death. She started to drift off, when there was a solid knock on the door. The sound jolted her awake, but Paul remained asleep.

She listened for a moment, wondering if the knock was part of a dream rather than reality, but the knock came again, seconds later. She wondered if it might be Kai, taking them up on the offer of a place to stay.

Sluggishly, she pulled herself up off the couch. As she reached the front door she felt a little strange, as if she was still half asleep. When she opened the door and saw Jason's expression, that feeling vanished, and she was suddenly sharply awake.

"What is it, Jason? What's wrong?" She guided him inside. Daylight had just begun to color the clouds in the sky. She had no idea what time it was, but she knew that if Jason was there, with that amount of strain on his face, it had to be about something important.

"I'm sorry, Suzie, I thought you should know right away, and since the investigation has already started I didn't want it to come as a surprise to you."

"It's okay, Jason, come in the kitchen with me. Everyone is still asleep. I'll start us some coffee."

"Thanks." Once they reached the kitchen he leaned heavily against the counter. She realized he hadn't slept at all.

"Summer has already started the examination. It turns out it wasn't an accident." He gazed at her. "We've opened a murder investigation. Which means I'm going to need to speak to both you and Paul, again. I'm going to have to interview everyone that had any contact with Ken. That includes your guests."

"I understand." Suzie shivered and wrapped her arms around herself as the coffee pot bubbled to life. "How do you know it wasn't an accident? What do you think happened to him?"

"We're not exactly sure, but Summer confirmed his neck didn't break from a fall. It was from a physical strike. Which means we're looking for someone strong. Unfortunately, that doesn't rule many people out. Half of the surfers in the group are strong enough to do that, and I'm sure a few members of the birdwatching group are as well."

"Sebastian and Tammy are trained in martial arts." Suzie's heart began to race. "But he's a small man." Suzie frowned. "Do you really think he could do something like that?"

"Size doesn't matter if you know how to cause harm. We don't think that there was much of a fight. I can't really tell you anything more than that." He glanced towards the stairs. "Do you think the guests will be coming down soon?"

"We serve breakfast at eight, but not everyone comes to it. Do you want me to call them down?"

"No, it's all right. I'm going to start with the surfers, then I'll come back here and hopefully everyone will be here for breakfast."

"I'll make sure there's some for you, too." She patted his shoulder. "I know this is going to be a tough case for you, Jason, make sure you don't overdo it." She poured him a cup of coffee in a travel mug, splashed some cream in it, and handed it over to him.

"Me?" He offered a light smile. "Would I ever do something like that?"

"Yes, you would."

"All right, I'll be back in a little bit." He wiped a hand across his eye.

As he stepped out through the door she stared after him. She knew how passionate he was about his work, he would often sacrifice his own health and well-being for the sake of a case. She just hoped that wouldn't be necessary in this instance. As she tucked herself back in close to Paul, strangely she felt calmer. At least now she knew why the pieces weren't adding up in her mind. Ken had been murdered, and even as disturbing as that was, she could finally drift off to sleep.

CHAPTER 6

When Suzie opened her eyes again, sunlight spilled through the front windows, and Paul was no longer on the couch. She heard the subtle sounds of someone in the kitchen. Still sleepy, but determined to wake up, she made her way to the kitchen.

"Oh Suzie, I hope I didn't wake you." Mary frowned as Suzie stepped into the kitchen. "I noticed that you made a pot of coffee so I figured you didn't get much sleep after I went to bed."

"No, I didn't. Jason stopped by with news about Ken's death." She grabbed the eggs from the refrigerator for Mary. "It's turned into a murder investigation."

"What?" Mary gasped. "Why?"

As Mary prepared breakfast, Suzie updated her

about the case. The more she talked, the more concerned she felt. She paused, and poured herself some coffee.

"So, they're certain it wasn't an accident?" Mary frowned. "How terrible. It was bad enough that he was killed, but to think that someone was right out there in those woods and did this to him. It makes me feel very uncomfortable."

"I understand. It was a shock to me, too. But Jason wants to interview our guests. I think it would be best if we just went through breakfast as normal, and then let Jason join us. If we tell anyone ahead of time we might interfere with the investigation."

"Okay." Mary shuddered. "Poor Ken. Just here on vacation, and then someone does this to him? I mean, I suppose it could have been anyone."

"I don't know, but I would imagine so. It seems to me that Ken might be the type to have some enemies." Suzie lowered her voice. "Jason said that it had to be someone strong who did this. Sebastian and Tammy are trained in martial arts, do you think that—"

"Sebastian?" Her eyes widened as she flipped the french toast in the pan. "No way. I mean, it's not like in the movies, right? Can martial arts training really make you capable of killing someone like that?"

"I don't know that much about it, but I do know that there are people who are highly trained. And Sebastian and Tammy seem to be very dedicated to it."

"That's true." Mary frowned. "But what motive could they have? Just because of a run-in with Ken in the woods?"

"I don't know. He definitely has a temper. Jason did say the surfers in the group had gotten into a fight at the local bar."

"Yes, and Ken had a problem with the organizer of the trip. Kai said that he had an argument with him, and then took off into the woods last night. That was probably the last time he was seen alive by anyone, but the killer." Mary glanced towards the stairs as she heard footsteps on them. She motioned for Suzie to be quiet.

Sebastian reached the bottom of the steps with Tammy right behind him.

"Sorry to interrupt. Tammy and I are just going to go out and do our training. We slept a little late this morning. But we'll be back in for breakfast." He nodded to them both as they walked past.

CINDY BELL

"Great, it'll be ready in about fifteen minutes." Mary smiled at them.

Suzie paid close attention to his hands, and fore-arms. If he'd gotten into a fight with Ken, there might be some evidence of the attack on his skin. However, from what she got a glimpse of she didn't see anything out of the ordinary.

A subtle nudge from Mary's hand drew her attention. Mary tipped her head in the direction of Tammy's elbow. It was scraped and slightly bruised. Suzie's heart skipped a beat. She hadn't really considered Tammy as an option, but now, she couldn't deny the possibility. She nodded to Mary as they both turned back to the stove.

As soon as she was sure they were out of earshot, Suzie leaned close to Mary.

"Do you think she could be involved?"

"I think she didn't have that scrape at dinner yesterday. At least not that I noticed." Mary flipped the french toast again.

"Suzie, I was hoping you'd sleep a bit longer." Paul stepped in through the side door. "I'm sure you didn't get enough rest."

"I got a little." She kissed his cheek. "Jason stopped by with an update." She shared with him the information that she'd been given, as well as what she and Mary noticed on Tammy's elbow.

"Interesting." Paul shook his head. "It's amazing how much can change overnight. But honestly, I wouldn't rule Kai out as a suspect."

"Kai?" Mary scooped the french toast onto a plate, then placed it in the oven to keep warm. "No way. He's a good kid. He would never do something like that."

"He's a good kid with an ax to grind against his father. I'm just saying, there is always a certain level of animosity between a father and son when the father has betrayed the mother. Wouldn't you agree, Mary?" He met her eyes, his expression soft, but his determination clear.

"I don't know about that, Paul. Ben, well both of my children, found ways to forgive their father, and I'm grateful for that."

"Are you sure they have?" Paul continued to study her. "Or is that just what they've told you?"

"Paul, it's probably not the best thing to bring up right now." Suzie placed her hand on the rise of his back. "Mary has gotten to know Kai, and if her instincts tell her he's not involved, I believe her. But that doesn't eliminate him as a suspect."

"Eliminate who as a suspect?" Bert stepped into

the kitchen from the stairs. "What's going on this morning?"

"Nothing really, just a private conversation." Suzie smiled. "I wasn't aware you were there."

"It's all right. I thought I'd sleep in later, but my stomach woke me." He patted his slender stomach, then approached the dining room.

"I'd better get breakfast on the table." Mary shot a brief glance in Paul's direction, then began to gather plates from the cabinet.

"I could use some fresh air. Paul, will you join me?" Suzie guided him towards the side door. She needed a break from the house and could sense that Mary needed a few minutes alone. She knew that Paul meant no harm with his comments, but she was also aware that Mary's marriage was still a raw topic with her. Not because she hadn't moved on from her ex, but because she still carried some guilt about her splintered family. Mary was more traditionally minded, and she'd confided in Suzie that it bothered her that even as adults her children were faced with a divorce. In Suzie's own life, relationships had come and gone so easily that she couldn't quite understand the heartbreak, but she didn't need to understand it in order to feel sympathy for her best friend, who she'd witnessed go through the most tumultuous time in her life.

❧

"*I*'m sorry, Suzie, did I say too much?" Paul turned to face her once they were on the beach.

"I don't think so, no, and I'm sure that Mary doesn't think so either. But she is still a little sensitive about the topic, it's probably not something she'd want to discuss in front of any guests." She wrapped her arm around his as her bare feet sank into the sand. The salt in the sea air refreshed her, but her heart was still heavy. "I just needed to get out of there. I don't know how the guests will react when we tell them that Ken was murdered, that it wasn't an accident."

"Do you really think one of them might have been involved?" He walked beside her as they approached the water.

"Honestly, if I was going to point a finger at anyone, it would be Sebastian. He's the one that got into it so intensely with Ken during the bird-watching excursion. He certainly seems to have just as much of a temper as Ken does, or did." She winced. "But Sebastian is so small. Bert is a possibility as well. But he is quite a bit older than us, and sure he's in good shape, but I'm not sure if he could kill a man like Ken with his bare hands. In fact, I'm pretty sure that he couldn't."

"It's easy to underestimate someone because of their age, but that's not always the best judge. I mean, I've known men who worked on boats into their nineties, and I would trust them more than I would trust any twenty-something that tried to take me out on the open water." He paused at the edge of the water and gazed out over the waves. "Experience is an incredible asset. The wisdom that comes with age is something that can't be learned from any text book."

"That's true, but in this case, we're talking about physical strength. I'm not saying that Bert isn't strong, but he's a relatively small man compared to Ken, I just don't see it happening." She sighed. "The truth is, it could be anyone. It could have just been someone he ran into in the woods. It could have been an enemy from his past. Apparently, Ken was a pretty wealthy businessman, and you and I both know that wealth doesn't always come easily. Sometimes it takes stepping on toes in order to achieve."

"Yes, you're right. Still, Ken was on vacation

here. If it was someone from his past, they would have to know that he was here, that they would have the opportunity to attack him, and that they would succeed without getting caught. That's a lot of unpredictability. I think your best suspect to start with is the leader of the camping trip. Noel. You know he argued with him. If this was a case of tempers getting out of control, then he had a good amount of motive to go after Ken." A shrill cry carried through the morning air. Paul's body snapped around in reaction to it. Suzie turned in time to see Sebastian with Tammy pinned down beneath him. He had his fist leveled towards her throat as if he was about to strike.

"Don't you dare!" Paul shouted and took off at a sprint towards Sebastian.

Suzie ran after him, but before either of them could reach Sebastian and Tammy, Sebastian had lowered his hand and offered it to Tammy. She jumped up to her feet, out of breath, her cheeks flushed.

Paul slammed his hands into Sebastian's chest and knocked him back a few steps.

"What were you about to do? You think you're tough, putting your hands on your wife?"

"No stop, please!" Tammy gasped out. "You've

misunderstood. Please, don't hurt him, Sebastian."
She looked past Paul, to her husband whose expression was tight with anger.

"Put your hands on me again and we're going to have a problem." Sebastian's tone was rough as he glared at Paul.

"We were just training, please calm down. I know how it must have looked to you, but Sebastian would never hurt me." Tammy stepped past Paul and wrapped her arms around her husband's waist. "Just take a breath, sweetie, he was only trying to protect me."

Sebastian drew a deep breath, then nodded. His body relaxed.

"I'm sorry, it's just when someone runs at me like that, sometimes it's hard for me to stay in control." He cleared his throat. "This is just a misunderstanding."

"I heard her scream, that was no misunderstanding." Paul's shoulders were still tense as if he might lash out at any moment.

Suzie stepped up beside him and rubbed his right arm, from elbow to wrist.

"I heard the scream, too, are you sure you're okay, Tammy?"

"Yes, that was my fault." She sighed. "I scraped

my arm yesterday when we were climbing on some rocks by the water. I forgot about it, and when Seb flipped me, I landed on it instead of my shoulder. It hurt more than I expected, I guess the sand got into some of the scrapes. I know better than to land on an injured area, but I was so caught up in the movement that I forgot until the pain hit. I'm sorry if I startled you both, and Paul, I understand why what you saw worried you, but Sebastian and I have been training together for a long time. We are both very respectful of each others' safety. I trust him, completely." She smiled as she looked into her husband's eyes. "I should have been more careful, Seb."

"I told you we shouldn't train until that heals, or at least you need to wear a wrap over it." He kissed her cheek, then inspected her elbow. "Yes, it looks like you've broken up the wound again."

"I have a first aid kit inside, why don't you let me clean you up, Tammy." Suzie glanced at Paul to make sure he was calm.

"I'm sorry about shoving you, Sebastian." Paul offered his hand. "It was just instinct."

"I understand." Sebastian shook his hand. "I'm sure I'd do the same if the situation was reversed. I appreciate you looking out for Tammy."

Suzie led Tammy into the house through the front door, relieved that Paul and Sebastian seemed to have settled things. But she couldn't shake the memory of Sebastian's fist angled at Tammy's throat. In that moment, she was certain that he was the killer. Now that the moment had passed, she still had to wonder just how easily Sebastian could be set off. If he ran into Ken in the woods and got into an argument, could he have lashed out and killed him?

"Thanks, Suzie." Tammy smiled as she followed her into the bathroom. "He's right, I should have wrapped it."

"I didn't realize you fell on the rocks." Suzie grabbed some ointment and bandages from the medicine cabinet. "They can be quite slippery."

"Yes, I was probably moving faster than I should have. I'm sorry for scaring you and Paul. You have a good man there, though, not many will go after Sebastian, especially after they've seen him in action."

"Paul is a brave guy." She dabbed Tammy's elbow with antiseptic. When she saw the woman wince she met her eyes. "Do you ever worry that Sebastian will lose his temper and hurt you? Or make a mistake?"

"No." She smiled. "He's a beautiful man, inside

and out. He would never hurt me. There have been times that I've seen him sparring with others and it's like he's a totally different man, that is a little shocking, but he's always careful. He's never injured anyone by mistake. His teacher stresses that control is absolutely the most important part of his training, and Sebastian has taught me the same way. If you're going to turn your body into a deadly weapon, then you must be in control of it and your emotions at all times."

"There." Suzie smoothed down the bandage and smiled. "No more getting tossed around in the sand, all right?"

"Nope, from now until this heals I'm going to be the one doing the tossing." She laughed.

Suzie smiled in return, but she still wondered if Tammy was telling the whole truth.

CHAPTER 7

"There you go, Bert." Mary placed a plate of french toast down in front of him. "Did you sleep well?"

"Very." He smiled. "Breakfast smells and looks delicious."

"Thank you. Cinnamon apple french toast is one of my favorites. I think it's great comfort food."

"Mm, I can't wait to taste it." He looked up as Callie descended the stairs into the kitchen.

"Morning Bert, Mary." She smiled at both of them as she approached the table. "I couldn't sleep any longer with that amazing aroma teasing me awake. Thanks for going to all the trouble, Mary."

"I am glad to be able to do it. I think we all need a nice warm meal this morning." She set a plate in

CINDY BELL

front of Callie. "Would you like some coffee, orange juice?"

"Some juice would be great. I think I'm too wound up for coffee."

"I'll get it right out to you. And Bert, coffee?"

"Yes, please." He looked across the table at Callie. "How are you holding up? You look like you didn't sleep much at all."

"It was tough. Herb and I were both upset."

As if summoned by her words, Herb made his way down the stairs to join them.

"Morning, Bert." He settled at the table across from him. "What a mess, huh? Are we going to continue with the trip?"

"Yes, I don't see a reason not to." Bert shrugged. "We've seen the Little Furn, I for one don't want to miss the chance to see it again, and properly this time."

"Seems like bad vibes after what happened to Ken." Herb frowned. "We've seen the bird, can't we just move on?"

"Seen, but we didn't get a picture." Callie glanced over at him. "I can't leave here without a picture."

"Right, maybe you can put that in your cage instead of that stuffed animal." Herb rolled his eyes.

"Morning, Herb." Mary interrupted them before the argument could escalate. "Here's some french toast for you. What would you like to drink?"

"I don't know, yet. I'll get something later. Thanks for this." He picked up his fork. "Looks good."

"Thanks." Mary smiled, then looked up as Suzie and Tammy approached the table. "Tammy, are you okay?" She stared at the bandage with concern.

"I'm fine, thanks. It's just from a slip on the rocks. Yesterday, Sebastian and I went out after dinner, and the rocks were slick. I didn't realize. Then I aggravated it this morning while we were training." She sat down on the other side of Callie. "I'll be fine in a day or two."

"Let me get you a plate. Coffee?" Mary offered.

"Tea, please."

"Coming right up."

Suzie followed her into the kitchen to help. As she did, Paul stepped in through the back door.

"Sebastian's going in through the front." Paul frowned. "Sorry if I overstepped, Suzie."

"You didn't at all." Suzie shared with Mary what happened on the beach.

"Oh my, that would have scared me." Mary frowned. "Training or not, that doesn't seem right."

"Maybe not, but Tammy says she trusts him completely." Suzie poured some tea into a cup. "To each their own, right?"

"Yes." Paul nodded. "I should head back to the dock, there are some things I need to do on the boat. But if you need anything just call me, okay?"

"Okay, I will. Thanks for everything, Paul." She gave him a quick kiss.

"For you." Mary handed him a travel mug of coffee and a container. "You can't miss out on this french toast, trust me."

"Thanks, Mary." He grinned at her.

After Paul stepped back out through the door, Suzie carried Tammy's tea out to her. Sebastian had settled beside Bert, and the two spoke quietly to each other.

"Sebastian, can I get you anything to drink?" Suzie met his eyes as she set Tammy's tea down in front of her.

"Just some coffee, please." He nodded.

"Sure thing." She passed Mary as she brought out a platter of french toast. Just then, the front door swung open and Jason stepped inside. Suzie met Mary's eyes briefly, then continued into the kitchen. Now it would be up to Jason to decide how much he would reveal and when he would reveal it.

"Morning everyone." Jason paused at the end of the table and placed his hands on the back of an empty chair. He stared down the length of the table. "I have some news about what happened last night."

All attention turned to him. Suzie could tell that he was uncomfortable, but she guessed that everyone else only saw a confident and authoritative man. She saw the tension in his knuckles as he gripped the chair. She heard the subtle waver in his voice that was normally not there. She even noticed that he held his shoulders straight. He only did that when he was expecting an argument. She'd gotten to know these little things about him, and now she wished that she could tell him that he could relax. But he couldn't, because it was his responsibility to solve this crime. A responsibility that he took very seriously.

"According to the medical examiner, Ken's death was not an accident as we'd first assumed. He was in fact, murdered."

A flurry of gasps and whispers carried around the table.

Mary did her best to assess the reaction of each of the guests. While Callie looked stunned, Herb seemed impatient and even took a bite of his french toast. Tammy stared hard at her plate, while Sebastian leaned forward and shifted the feet of his chair. The subtle scraping sound filled the silence that followed everyone's initial reaction. Bert remained still in his chair, gazing straight ahead, but his chin trembled some. She wondered if he could be regretting the way he had spoken about Ken.

"I know this is a shock. I know that it may make you feel unsafe. We are doing our very best to figure out exactly what happened and bring the killer to justice, but it will take us some time. If you can think of anything that might help the investigation, something you might have seen or heard, please do not hesitate to contact me." Jason cleared his throat. "I am going to need to speak to each of you individually, since you all had contact with Ken. I will do my best to keep the interviews brief, and please understand that even if you don't think you know anything, answering a few questions could certainly help this investigation. I would appreciate your cooperation."

"Absolutely." Bert set down his fork and looked directly at Jason. "Anything you might need, we're all available. Right?" He glanced around at the others in the group.

After a few nods from the others, Herb spoke up.

"Let me get this straight. Not only are we expected to deal with the fact that someone was murdered not even a mile away from us, but now we have to be part of a police investigation? That doesn't sound like a very good vacation to me." He shook his head. "I had nothing to do with Ken, and I have nothing to say about him."

"Why don't you just enjoy your breakfast, Herb, we can talk about all of this when you're done. All right?" Mary smiled. "More coffee?"

"It's okay, Mary. I know this is difficult. But once it's done, it's done," Jason said.

"We're all just a little tired, Jason, I'm sure that Herb will be happy to help you with the investigation." Bert picked up his fork again. "But yes, we should all eat." He shot Mary a soft smile. "After all, a lot of love went into this breakfast."

Mary smiled in return. Bert might have had a bit of a temper when it came to Ken, but he certainly knew how to calm things down when he wanted to.

*A*fter breakfast was finished, Jason took each guest one by one into the study to interview them. Once the guests were finished, he poked his head out and called Suzie in.

"Is Paul here, yet?"

"No, he texted me that he's running behind. But he did say if you want to meet him at the boat you can. He had some trouble with it this run. I think the repairs are a bit more involved than he anticipated."

"Okay thanks, that's fine, I'll go down there to speak to him." He gestured to a chair beside him. "Let's just talk for a minute."

"Sure, anything I can do to help." She rested her hands in her lap and gazed at him. "I know how hard this must be on you, Jason."

"I'm doing okay. I'm more worried about you, and Mary." He glanced towards the door, then back to her. "Do you think someone here might have had something to do with this?"

"Not really. I mean, there was a run-in between Ken and the group. It got quite heated, but there wasn't much to it. Just a bit of back and forth over a bird. Nothing that anyone would kill over."

"That's your opinion." He nodded. "But people

can be very unpredictable. I wonder if you could tell me anything about the people staying here. Have you overheard or witnessed anything that concerned you?"

"Well, nothing related to Ken I don't think." Suzie frowned.

"Anything at all, I'd like to know about it." He glanced up from his notepad.

"Well, there is some tension between Callie and Herb. He's a bit mean to her, always putting her down." She shrugged. "I hate to say that. It's not like I know them well. But from what I've seen, they don't get along."

"Interesting, okay." He nodded as he jotted down a note. "Anything else?"

"Well, this morning Sebastian and Tammy were out practicing martial arts, and when Sebastian pinned her down, I don't know, just the way he held his fist above her, it just made my blood run cold. Paul almost knocked him out for it." She pursed her lips. "But Tammy says it's all part of training and that she trusts Sebastian not to hurt her."

"Hmm, I'm sure there are some specific strikes in martial arts that can deliver the kind of blow that killed Ken. I'll have to look into that. Although, a few of the surfers also practice, so it certainly

doesn't narrow things down. Thanks for the information, Suzie. I'll do my best to keep you up
to date."

"Thanks, Jason. And please, try to get
some rest."

"I'll try." He flashed her a brief smile as she
stepped out of the study.

"Is he ready for me?" Mary walked towards her.

"Yes, I think so. How is everyone out here?"

"They've scattered. I don't think anyone wants
to be here right now." She sighed. "No amount of
sprucing is going to clean up the memory of what's
happened."

"It's all right, Mary, once Jason figures out who
did this, everything will calm down." She looked
into her eyes. "Have you heard from Wes?"

"Yes, he's on his way here. I told him he didn't
have to come, but he insisted." She smiled some.
"It'll be nice to see him. I'd better get in there, I
don't want to hold Jason up."

She headed for the study just as Jason opened
the door. He held it open for her, then settled in
a chair.

"Hi Mary, thanks for talking with me." He
smiled as she sat down across from him. "I know

there's a lot going on right now, you probably have a lot on your mind."

"It's all right. If I can do anything to help, I will. The only problem is, I'm not sure that I can help."

"Have you noticed anything unusual about the guests. Or maybe any interactions you've had with the surfers on the beach?"

"Nothing unusual, no. I mean, I do know that Ken had a run-in with Noel, the organizer of the camping trip. But Ken just seemed to have a bit of a temper in general and antagonized the people he met."

"Did you notice anyone else hanging around the beach or the woods? Maybe even the house? Someone unfamiliar?"

"Not at all." She shook her head. "But I don't know all of the people in the surf group, so it's possible that someone could have easily blended in."

"Thanks, Mary. If I need anything else, I'll be in touch. For now, just do your best to keep your eyes and ears open, okay? Anything you hear or see, don't hesitate to reach out to me. Although, it is very possible that a stranger committed the murder, at this point we are focusing on the killer being someone that Ken knew. So, chances are that you have seen or spoken to the person who did this."

"That's an eerie thought." She winced.

"I know it is. I believe there is a strong possibility that the suspect is still in the area. I want both you and Suzie to be careful. All right?"

"Yes, we will be. Thank you for telling me." She patted his hand. "I know that you'll get to the bottom of this quickly, Jason."

"Thank you, Mary. I hope so." Jason smiled slightly as they stepped out of the study together.

CHAPTER 8

After Mary was finished with Jason she caught sight of Wes near the front door. Her heartbeat quickened at the sight of him. Her cheeks flushed with heat. Despite the fact that she saw him quite often, she still felt a little thrill the first moment she laid eyes on him. It made her feel silly, and awkward, but she was also grateful that she'd been able to connect with him.

"Mary!" He walked over to her and opened his arms. "I'm so glad to see you. When I heard the news, I wanted to come right away, but I was in the middle of a case. I'm sorry."

"There's no need to apologize, you did the right thing. There's not much you can do here." She hugged him, then met his eyes. "Okay, I take that back, there's a lot you can do. Thanks for being here."

"It's my pleasure." He kissed her forehead. "I just wish that I could get this settled for you."

"I don't think that Jason has a lot to go on."

"Maybe we can fix that." He took her hand and led her out onto the side porch. After a quick glance around, he turned his attention back to her. "I did some digging."

"You did?" Her eyes widened. "Are you allowed to do that?"

"I wanted to know what you might be dealing with, especially now that it's been proven that Ken's death wasn't an accident." He lowered his voice. "I found out some information about both Ken and Kai."

His expression was stern, as if he had to convince himself to share the information. She knew that he was likely instructed not to get involved in the investigation, since he worked as a detective in the next town. She also knew from experience that he would do whatever he thought was right, even if that meant bucking direct orders.

"You should sit down. I know from Jason that you've taken an interest in Kai, and there is quite a bit to this story." He gestured to a nearby chair.

She held her breath for a moment as she wondered what he might have discovered. She hoped it would solve the case, but she sensed that there was something much more foreboding about the information.

"What is it?" She perched on the edge of a chair and watched as he began to pace back and forth.

"Ken is fairly well known in some exclusive circles. But so is his temper. There are stories about him clashing with several well-off people, but these types of people like to keep their names out of the newspapers, so no reports were filed." He paused in front of her. "Except for one. It was filed by his son, Kai. He accused his father of being aggressive towards him, and his mother. The charges were later dropped, but because Kai made an official report, there is a record of it."

"Kai actually turned his father in to the police? What did Ken do to his ex?" Mary frowned.

"According to the report, it was a matter of verbal hostility. He didn't place his hands on her, but he was acting in a threatening manner. The charges were dropped because Kai's mother refused to participate in the investigation, and Kai later recanted. He claimed he made up the whole thing."

"Do you think that's true?" She caught his hand

and pulled him closer to her. "Isn't it possible that Kai was just upset about the divorce and tried to make it seem like his father was out of control?"

"Sure, it's possible. That does happen now and then. But with Ken's reputation, it's hard to believe that there wasn't some truth to Kai's accusations. The point is, there was more than just resentment between these two. It got so bad that Kai went to the police about it, and seeing his father get away with that, couldn't have been easy for him."

"Maybe Kai didn't come here to reconnect at all. Maybe he came here to confront his father once and for all. They could have gotten into a vicious fight that ended in Ken's death." She tightened her grasp on his hand. "But he seems so nice, and kind. I wonder if he could even be capable of something like that."

"People are capable of far more than we ever give them credit for. You're the one who has met Kai, I trust your opinion. Do you really think he isn't capable of this?" He studied her expression.

"I can't be certain. I think my judgment is a little clouded. He reminds me in so many ways of my own son." She lowered her eyes. "I don't want to believe that he could have done it, but the truth is,

I'm not sure. He might just have been angry enough to do it."

"Kai has his own history. Did he tell you about that?" He brushed her hair back from her cheek as she looked back up at him.

"No, he didn't mention anything."

"He's been arrested for assault. Against his father."

"What?" Her eyes widened.

"Ken didn't press the charges himself. The altercation took place at a restaurant and the owner of the restaurant insisted on the arrest. But Ken later managed to get the charges dropped. So, Kai does have a history of attacking his father."

"And his father may have a history of attacking Kai." She sighed. "If he did this and he is caught, his life is over."

"All I know for sure is that there is bad blood between the two of them, enough that I could see something like this happening."

"But Ken was so much bigger than Kai. I just don't know."

"It's okay, you don't have to know. But it's a place to start." He glanced over his shoulder as Sebastian climbed the steps onto the porch.

"Mary, how are you?" He smiled at her, then

glanced at Wes and thrust his hand out. "I'm Sebastian."

"Sebastian, nice to meet you. I'm Wes." Wes grimaced a bit as he shook it.

"Have you seen Tammy? Herb wants us all to get together in the living room and decide what our next steps are going to be."

"Next steps?" Mary shook her head. "No, I haven't seen her since breakfast, I think she spoke to Jason already."

"Yes, we both did. I'll see if I can find her." He brushed past her with no further explanation. As he pulled the door shut behind him, Mary turned towards Wes.

"What do you think he means by that?"

"I'm not sure, but I can tell you that he has some grip." He rubbed his hand with the palm of his opposite hand. "A little tighter and he would have left bruises."

"He practices martial arts, maybe he doesn't realize how strong he is?" She stroked his hand with a delicate touch. "Are you okay?"

"Yes, I'm fine. It just seems a little unusual to me that a man who works with his body wouldn't know its strength. You go in ahead, I've got some things I'm going to check up on." He pulled her close for a quick kiss. "Sorry to leave so fast, but I'll be in touch."

"It's okay, I understand." She watched him head for the parking lot, then stepped back into the house. She was just in time to see all the guests gathered in the living room, with Herb as the center of attention. In the same moment that she entered the living room, Suzie entered from the hallway. They were at opposite ends of the room, but met eyes. Mary could sense that Suzie was just as concerned as she was. If all the guests decided to leave it would not only be a blow to their business, but a big issue for the investigation.

∿

*H*erb glanced at the others gathered around him as he stood in the center of the living room.

"I think all of us have had our interrogations now, haven't we?"

Suzie tensed up at the mention of interrogation. She was sure that Jason had been polite, but he could get quite intense, especially if he thought he was on to something. Had he been a bit too aggressive with Herb?

"What's this all about, Herb?" Bert sat forward in his chair and stared at Herb from beneath bushy, gray eyebrows. "Are you going to get to the point?"

"I just want to be sure that everyone is listening." He looked pointedly in Suzie's direction, then Mary's, before he continued. "I think we should leave." Herb looked straight at Callie. "There's no reason to stay here. Someone was murdered, just down the beach from here." He shook his head. "How can any of us feel secure enough to sleep here?"

"Herb, murders happen everywhere. Yes, it's terrible, but that's no reason for us to just run off. I want to see that Little Furn and get a photo of it, and if I give up my chance now, I will always regret it." Callie glanced over at Suzie and Mary. "It's not as if it was just some random killer, right? Someone was after Ken specifically. We're not in any danger."

"The police do not believe it was random, no. But until they know for certain who did it, there is some degree of danger to consider. I don't want to dismiss your concerns, but we keep Dune House secure, especially at night, and since Jason is here quite frequently, the police presence will help scare off anyone with bad intentions." Suzie clasped her hands in front of her.

"Except it didn't scare the killer off, did it? Just a few steps down from the beach Ken was murdered. I don't think the killer was worried about being caught." Herb frowned.

"Maybe he wasn't." Sebastian spoke up, with Tammy's hand clasped in his own. "Maybe he had a bone to pick with that arrogant jerk. I mean really, are any of us surprised that Ken was killed?" He glanced around at his friends. "He had our blood boiling, didn't he? I'm sure we're not the first ones that he's picked fights with."

"Sebastian, that's a little harsh." Tammy frowned as she pulled her hand away from his. "I barely knew the guy, but I'm sure he didn't deserve to die."

"I'm not saying that he did." He balled his hands into fists. "I'm just saying that I can see how it would happen. He wasn't a friendly person, and seemed to think he was in charge. If you cross the wrong person with that kind of attitude, you never know what will happen."

"Great, I hope you told the cop that, so that he'll come back here and slap cuffs on you, Seb!" Herb rolled his eyes. "Why don't you just paint a target on your back?"

"Keep quiet, Herb." Sebastian stood up from the couch and glared at him. "All you want to do is cut and run like a coward. I'm not afraid to stand my ground. I can take anyone who wants to take a shot at me."

"Are you trying to start something with me?" Herb glared back at him.

"Sebastian, sit down." Bert's voice was quiet, but so sharp that it sent a shiver down Mary's spine. When she looked across the room at Suzie, her expression had grown tense. Did she sense the same command in Bert's tone?

Suzie braced herself, as she expected that Sebastian would turn on Bert next. Instead, he sat down without speaking another word. He grabbed Tammy's hand again, and this time she didn't pull away. Bert stood up slowly from his chair and walked over to Herb.

"I understand your concerns, Herb. But I think you're overreacting. We came here for a reason, and we will be able to complete our trip if we just allow the police to do their work." He rested a hand lightly on Herb's shoulder. "You're upset, I get it, we all are."

"Yes, I'm upset." Herb stared back at him. "Upset that none of you have any common sense." He brushed Bert's hand away, then turned back to his wife. "Callie, I'll give you another day to see that stupid bird, but after that we're out of here. Understand?"

"Herb, we've already paid, and Bert has come all of this way just for this and —"

"And nothing." Herb took a step closer to her. "One more day, that's it."

"Be reasonable, Herb, this is clearly important to Callie." Bert gave him a light pat on his back. "Let's just sleep on it and see how we all feel tomorrow, all right?"

"Why don't you just mind your own business, Bert?" He shot him a glare, then stomped towards the stairs.

"Herb!" Callie called after him as he headed up the stairs. He didn't bother to look back and disappeared across the landing. "Oh dear." She wiped at her eyes as tears began to fall. "He can be so stubborn. I've been waiting so long for this, and now he's going to ruin it for me."

"Don't be upset, Callie." Bert took a few steps towards her, then gestured to Tammy. "Listen, everything's going to be fine."

"Sure, it is." Tammy smiled as she sat down beside Callie, then wrapped her arm around her shoulders. "I know that it seems bleak right now, but by tomorrow Herb will have calmed down and we'll all get back to normal. All right?"

"Yes, thank you, Tammy." She glanced up at Bert. "I'm so sorry he was rude to you, Bert. You've done so much for us."

"Don't worry about Herb, I'm used to him. It's you I'm worried about." He looked into her eyes. "Don't let anything get you down. You can still enjoy your trip if you try."

"I will try." She offered a fragile smile as she held his gaze. "After all that you did to get us here, I promise, I will try."

"That's all I want to hear." He nodded to her, looked once in the direction of the stairs, then stood up and headed for the door. "I'm going to go for a walk." As he walked past Mary, he paused, and met her eyes. "Don't let Herb bother you, either. He likes to act like a tough guy all of the time, but he's really harmless."

"I'll keep that in mind." She spared him a brief smile, but her attention was focused on Sebastian. His temper had grown short very quickly. Had it grown short with Ken and led to murder?

CHAPTER 9

Suzie gestured for Mary to join her out on the porch. She was cautious to discuss too much inside the house.

"That was strange." Mary frowned as she leaned against the railing beside Suzie. "I thought Herb was really going to lose it."

"I thought he did lose it." She shook her head. "Can you believe he talked to Callie that way?"

"Yes." She grimaced. "Marriage can have moments like that."

"Right, I'm sorry, Mary, that was insensitive of me. I guess it still shocks me when I see it in person."

"There's nothing to apologize for. Herb seems very volatile. He would never stand a chance against Sebastian."

"You know I thought birdwatchers would be mellow, laid back people. Didn't you?" She shook her head.

"I guess anyone who has that much passion can be a little temperamental?" Mary cracked a smile.

"Maybe." After a moment's thought, Suzie glanced towards the door. "Can you hold down the fort for a little while? There's someone I want to go have a conversation with."

"Yes, absolutely. Who are you going to talk to?"

"Someone else, who has quite a bit of passion." Suzie explained where she was going, patted her friend on the shoulder, then walked to the beach. She headed in the direction of the campsite and spotted the person she wanted to talk to. Luckily, he was sitting alone beside the fire. It looked as if he might have just started it.

"Noel, right?" Suzie smiled as she sat down on a log beside the fire. "Can I speak with you for a moment?"

"Sure." He looked over at her. "Not many people are."

"No?" She raised an eyebrow. "Why not?"

"Everyone knows that I got into an argument with Ken last night. The police have been all over me with questions, so of course everyone in my tour group is now looking at me strangely, wondering if I'm a killer." He eyed her for a moment. "Kind of like the way you're looking at me right now."

"I'm not." She lowered her eyes as a rush of heat flooded her cheeks. Was she? She certainly wanted to know if he was a killer or not. "I just thought you might have some insight into what happened. What was Ken really like?"

"What you see is what you get with Ken. He was nothing but trouble. He was obnoxious, and short-tempered. I know." He held up his hands. "I should lay it on thick about how he was this great guy, and it was such a tragedy, but I'm sorry, the man I knew was nothing short of a jerk. He had plenty of money, but questioned every penny he had to spend on this trip. He was so stubborn. He argued about the bad surf conditions, even though he wouldn't listen to me that he needed to go when the tide was high. We also argued because he expected me to provide him meals and drinks on the trip. I never offered that, but he insisted I did. His poor son." He shook his head. "The kid is never going to live any of this down."

"About Kai, did you ever notice him and his father fighting?" She leaned a little closer to him.

"Yes, on more than one occasion. Sparks were

flying between those two from the moment they boarded the bus to come here. I picked them and a few other members of the group up at the airport and I noticed the heat between them right away. Kai didn't say a word, but he didn't have to, the way his father looked at him, it made it clear that the two had issues." He picked up a pebble from the sand and tossed it into the fire. "How great of a guy can you be if your own son wants nothing to do with you?"

"It sounds like you might know a little bit more about the situation. Did Kai tell you what the issues were between him and his father?" She dug her toes into the sand and returned her attention to the fire. She wanted the conversation to remain casual, otherwise Noel might start to clam up.

"Just that he only came for the free trip. After Ken stirred up a fight in one of the local bars, Kai apologized to me, and said that he knew his father was out of control. He told me why he came along, and that if there were any more issues he would do whatever he could to help me. I was pretty upset at that point and told him the best thing he could do was—"

He suddenly stopped talking. His eyes grew wide in the glow of the flames.

"Noel? What is it? Are you okay?" She stared hard at him.

"I told him, the best thing he could do was get rid of his father." He shifted his gaze to her, his eyes still wide. "I didn't mean it like that though, I swear I didn't."

"It's all right, Noel. You were upset. I'm sure Kai understood." She tilted her head to the side as she studied him. She'd come there to find out more about him, and they only ended up talking about Kai. Had he made sure the conversation steered that way? Was he trying to deflect any attention towards Kai in an attempt to pin the murder on him?

"What made you start these surfing tours, Noel?"

He relaxed a little and looked back at the fire. "Honestly, I was lonely."

"I'm sorry?" His comment held her attention.

"I was single, I had just turned forty, and I had no friends. I'd left my wife, left my job, and moved to a new place. It is not easy to make friends as an adult. I loved to surf, but I couldn't break into the tight knit local group. I noticed a few other stragglers on the beach. I thought about how nice it would be to have a surfing group, just a bunch of people with a shared interest. Then I thought about all of the places I dreamed about surfing, and the idea kind of came together. I thought it would be a hit, and it has gone pretty well. I'm not getting rich or anything, but I get to do what I love, meet new people, and travel. I can't complain about that. It's probably the best decision I ever made."

"That was pretty brave of you to make such a big change." Suzie gestured over her shoulder towards Dune House. "When I first reopened the bed and breakfast I was sure it wouldn't do much. But it took off pretty quickly. Is that how it was for you?"

"At first. It got even better when I got great reviews on this travel website. But the interest grows and fades at different times. It's a bit of a struggle to keep things afloat to be honest, but as long as I can still do it, I will continue." He met her eyes. "I guess you know it's not great for business to have somebody murdered on your watch."

"It's not your fault, you know. Whatever happened to Ken, he chose to go into the woods on his own." She tried to read his emotions in his expression, but it remained passive as he gazed at the growing fire.

"Did he? Or maybe our argument drove him off. He threatened me again, and I'd had enough. I told him he would have to leave the tour the next morning and that if he didn't I would get the police involved. Now, I wonder, if I had just kept my mouth shut, maybe he would still be alive. Maybe Kai would still have his father." He glanced at her, then looked back at the fire. "I didn't kill him, Suzie, but that doesn't mean I didn't play a part in his death." He stood up and headed down the beach. Suzie thought about following him, but decided against it. Though he claimed not to be the killer, she couldn't be certain about that, and his last words left her even more unsettled. Did he play more of a part in Ken's death than he was admitting? Could he have sent someone after his problem guest?

As she walked back to the house she thought about something that Noel said. He mentioned a travel website that posted reviews about his surfing group. She decided to hunt down the site and read the reviews for herself. When she got back to the house she settled on the porch instead of going inside. She searched 'Noel's Surfing Tours', the name of the surfing tour company, as well as Noel Penning, Noel's full name. It didn't take long for her to find the travel site that hosted the reviews. As Noel had said, most of the reviews were glowing. Then she came across one of the most recently posted reviews. It was posted by Ken, and he did not mince words about just how terrible he thought Noel and the tour were. He accused Noel of being a con artist and warned others not to waste their money on the tour.

~

There wasn't much to do in the house, as everyone kept to themselves in their rooms. Mary busied herself with some light cleaning and tried not to think about the meeting in the living room. She knew that a mass exodus of guests wouldn't be great for their reputation, but more than that it would be a personal blow to both herself and Suzie, as they prided themselves on creating a safe, happy environment for their guests. So far it did not feel that they had succeeded in doing that. When she heard footsteps on the porch she looked out through the window. Suzie sat in one of the chairs outside, her brows furrowed, and her lips tense.

"Suzie?" Mary stepped outside. "Are you okay? You look worried."

"Take a look at this." She held out her phone to Mary, who took it from her. "I found a website that

Noel mentioned, and apparently not long before Ken was killed he posted that review."

"Wow, this is pretty harsh. He calls Noel a con artist, and says the tour is a complete rip off. He gets more personal by saying Noel is stupid and that he has no idea how to run a tour. He even blames him for bad surfing conditions." She winced. "That's a pretty bad review. And it's gotten several views."

"A bad review that Noel never mentioned." Suzie raised an eyebrow. "Why do you think that is?"

"I don't know, maybe he never saw it. Maybe he was embarrassed."

"That's possible. He said he started the tours to make friends, that he was a lonely guy before this. If he is a sensitive guy then this could be an especially big blow to his reputation."

"Yes, it could be, and Ken's wealth and influence could devastate a small tour like Noel's." She lowered the phone and met Suzie's eyes. "It might even be enough to make him want to hurt Ken."

"My thoughts exactly. I'm willing to bet that argument that night was about that review. Maybe Noel let him go into the woods, then waited a few minutes and went in another way. Maybe he thought he could surprise him, and attack him." She took her phone back and began to type out a text. "I'm going to send a link to this review to Jason. I'm sure he'll be interested in it."

"I'm sure he will be, too, but I'm not so sure about Noel being the killer." Mary frowned. "Do you think he's physically strong enough to pull off something like that?"

"Honestly, I never really paid that much attention to how strong he might be. He seems like a fit guy, and he's a surfer. I guess the question is how much strength would be needed to cause the kind of injury that killed Ken."

"Yes, that would be good to know." She frowned. "Did you see Kai down at the beach at all? I haven't seen him out there much."

"No, I didn't. Why?" She met Mary's eyes.

"Just curious about how he's doing." Mary shrugged. "I want to see if he's okay."

Suzie grabbed Mary's hand for a moment, and continued to study her. "We don't know if he was involved in this or not, Mary. From what Noel said, Kai really disliked his father. He has more motive than anyone else. You need to be careful."

"I will be, I promise. I'll just walk along the beach and see if I can find him." She lingered a moment longer and gave Suzie a smile of reassurance. "Don't worry, I'll be fine."

As Mary headed down the steps and out onto the sand she tried to believe her own words. She knew how tense things could be between feuding family members, and Kai was at an age where kids were often trying to figure out where they belong, which could lead to acting out and destructive behavior. The beach was quiet, which was unusual for such a nice day. She guessed that most of the surfers from the campsite had chosen to stay away for the day, and other locals that might enjoy the beach had likely heard the story about Ken's death. It wasn't easy to relax or have fun knowing that someone had been killed not far away. Over time, the stigma would fade, but for now the beach felt abandoned. At least until she saw a figure gliding across the rolling waves. She gazed at the young man who stood out against the sun, mastering the wild ocean beneath him. Was he a killer?

CHAPTER 10

*A*fter a few minutes Kai swam into the shore. He walked towards Mary.

"I spotted you out there surfing. You were doing great." She watched as he tossed his surfboard down in the sand.

"It didn't feel great." He frowned and wiped the wet hair away from his forehead. "I keep going out there hoping to just have a moment of peace. I think if I can just catch a really good wave, then I'll be able to forget, just for a second. But it doesn't happen." He met her eyes. "I can't forget."

"I'm so sorry, Kai. I can't imagine how terrible this is for you. Were you able to get hold of your mother?" She walked beside him as he headed back towards the campsite.

"Yes, she'll be here in a little while. Thanks for

telling me to call her. You were right. She was concerned about me. She got me a lawyer."

"A lawyer?" Mary paused in the sand as he neared the campsite.

"Yes." He turned back to face her. "The cops are trying to pin my father's murder on me." He shrugged. "It's to be expected I guess."

"Why would you say that?" She crossed the distance between them.

"My father and I had a lot of issues when he broke things off with my mom. His temper, you know. He was shouting at her, and it was upsetting her, so I started shouting at him. I thought I was being tough. It was just a mess. Then after the divorce, he invited me to dinner to meet the woman he was cheating on my mom with. Only, I didn't know that. He said we were going to have dinner. I thought it was just the two of us. I thought we were finally going to hash things out." He sighed and brushed his hair back again. "But that's not what happened. She was there, and he tried to smooth things over like it was okay what he did to my mom because he was in love with this new woman. In love, can you believe it?" He rolled his eyes. "So we argued, and I lost it. I shoved him, and I punched him." He lowered his eyes. "It was stupid. I shouldn't have done it. But he was sitting there, so smug, with this girl that was like four years older than me, talking about love, and I just couldn't take it." He glanced up at her. "I don't know why I'm telling you all of this. I guess I need one person here to know that yes, I had problems with my father, and yes I was arrested for attacking him in that restaurant, but no I didn't kill him. He was still my dad. I wouldn't do that."

"I understand, Kai," Mary said as Kai dried off. "I know how difficult it must have been for you during the divorce. My own children went through it, and they were not much older than you at the time. It is a very emotional experience, and you were trying to figure it all out. I'm sure your father understood that."

"I hope so." His jaw locked as he put on a t-shirt and shoes. "But honestly, I'm not so sure if I care if he did or not. If it wasn't for him, we wouldn't have even been on this trip. He was always trying to smooth things over, or sweep them under the rug. He never wanted to have a real conversation."

"Kai!" A shrill voice hollered from further up the beach.

He spun around, then waved to the woman who

approached, heels in one hand and a briefcase in the other as she teetered across the sand.

"That's my mom."

"I would love to meet her." Mary matched his pace as he approached her. "If you don't mind."

"I don't." He smiled at her. "You've been so kind to me, Mary."

A ripple of guilt carried through her as she smiled at him in return. Was it kind of her to suspect that he might be involved in his father's death? She wasn't convinced that he wasn't, and yet he was relying on her as the one person who believed he was innocent.

"Mom!" He threw his arms around his mother, who embraced him in return. The briefcase dropped out of her hand and fell into the sand.

Mary scooped it up and as they pulled away from the hug, she offered it back to her.

"Who's this?" She took the briefcase from her, then looked at her son.

"Her name is Mary. She runs the bed and breakfast over there." He pointed in the direction of Dune House. "She's been very kind to me."

"Son, I told you, be careful who you speak to. You never know who someone actually is." She shot a look in Mary's direction. "Thank you for helping Kai. I'm Lisa." She offered her hand.

"It's no problem." She shook her hand. "You have a wonderful son, and I'm terribly sorry for your loss."

"Not my loss." She frowned. "The world is a better place without Ken in it. Let's go, Kai, we need to get you cleaned up before we meet with the lawyer." She steered her son away from the campsite, and Mary. "I brought with your suit." She pointed to a suitcase that stood in the direction she had come from. "I couldn't carry everything."

Startled by her harsh words, Mary stared after them. She could understand why there was no love lost between Lisa and Ken, but the comment seemed very insensitive to her son's feelings. Then again, maybe she was right, maybe the world was a better place without him.

～

On Mary's way back towards the house, a familiar voice called out to her.

"Mary! Mary, can I speak to you!"

She turned and saw Bert jogging towards her from the edge of the woods. A flush of fear stopped her in her tracks. Why had he been in the woods? Beyond him, she caught sight of Tammy and Sebastian who were practicing some of their movements several feet away from the woods.

"Yes of course, Bert. How are you?"

"I'm doing the best I can." He paused in front of her.

"I understand." She noticed that he hadn't even broken into a sweat as he ran. He was in good shape.

"Do you have any idea how long they're going to have that area roped off?" Bert crossed his arms as he looked back towards the trail.

"Once they've processed all of the evidence from the area I'm sure they'll clear it." She studied the tension in his jaw and his arms. "Is that a problem?"

"Yes, of course it is. That's near the area where we spotted the Little Furn. If we have any chance of finding it, it's going to be there. But now we're not allowed to walk that trail."

"I see." She looked past him, towards the trail. It was hard for her to believe that he would want to explore an area where someone had recently died, but then she knew he was determined to see the bird. "I'll talk to Jason and see if I can get an estimate on when they might be done. All right?"

"That would be great." He nodded, then turned back towards Tammy and Sebastian as they rounded each other in anticipation of a spar. "I'm trying to salvage what's left of this trip."

"I understand. How are the other members holding up?" She looked towards Sebastian and Tammy as well. "Are they handling everything okay?"

"As best as they can. Callie is a wreck, but she's a sensitive woman. Tammy and Sebastian, they usually keep to themselves, and as you can see their focus is often on training." He watched as they began to move together. "Beautiful, isn't it?"

"Yes." Mary studied what looked like a ballet of gestures between the two. "Although, it can be a little frightening, too. Were Sebastian or Tammy involved in a fight at the bar in Garber?"

"Tammy and Sebastian?" He laughed. "Not a chance. They are extremely disciplined. As far as I know they never even went to the bar. But I did hear some of the surfers were causing trouble there."

"Yes, me too." She pursed her lips. "Ken, especially."

"Doesn't surprise me. The guy had a bad attitude." He tipped his head towards the trail. "Anything you can do to get a rush on that, would be appreciated."

"I'll do what I can." She smiled, then turned back towards the house. The last thing she wanted to do was get caught up in a discussion about Ken's behavior. She already knew Bert's opinion of him and it wasn't a pleasant one. She was almost to the house when she spotted Kai and Lisa on the porch. It surprised her that they had returned so quickly. She waved as she walked up to them. She noticed Suzie step out of the house. When Mary joined them on the porch, Kai looked at her with a hint of nervousness in his expression.

"Can my mom and I get rooms here please? We were going to check in at the motel, but she doesn't like it there." He rolled his eyes. "She's a little picky."

"Sure, of course you can, free of charge." Mary glanced over at Suzie.

"Yes, absolutely." Suzie nodded. "I'll get you some keys." She ducked into the house.

"Are you sure you don't mind?" Kai frowned. "I know there's a lot of suspicion around me."

"Careful, Kai." Lisa glared at him.

"Don't worry about that." Mary smiled as Suzie stepped back out onto the porch. She had a tray of drinks and snacks for them, which she had already prepared for the other guests.

"Here are some snacks for you." She placed them on the table and held out the keys to them. "Here you go. The rooms are side by side on the third floor. We don't have anyone staying up there right now, so you'll have it to yourselves. Will that be okay for you?"

"Yes, perfect. Thanks so much. I may still camp out on the beach, but it'll be good to have the option."

"Why would you want to camp out on the beach when you could have a nice roof over your head?" Lisa shook her head. "I don't understand that." She grabbed a few crackers from the plate.

"It's peaceful out there, Mom. You should try it sometime."

"No thanks. I like a real bed, in a real house. That's my ideal." She sighed, then looked at her son. "You're still young, though."

"That's what you always say. Maybe it's not because I'm young, maybe I just have my own opinions?"

"The beach can be a very soothing place." Suzie smiled, and hoped to break the tension between the two. "Is there anything else you two need while you're staying here?"

"There is one thing. I just need to get my mom to a car rental place. We were going to go there before we got a room here. So, we called for a taxi twenty minutes ago, but no one has shown up." Kai squinted at the sky. "It's getting late, we don't want to have to wait much longer."

"I can take you." Suzie smiled. "There's a rental place in town, it's not too far from here."

"Really?" He stared at her. "You don't mind?"

"Not at all, I was headed into town anyway, I need to pick up some things. That okay with you, Mary? If I take off for a bit?" She looked over at her friend.

"Yes, I can handle things here. Don't forget eggs!" Mary headed towards the door that led into the house.

"I won't!" Suzie made a note on her phone, as she guessed that she just might forget the eggs after all.

"This is extremely nice of you, Suzie." Lisa studied her, with a hint of skepticism in her voice.

"It's the least I can do." She frowned as she glanced over at Kai. "I'm just so sorry for your loss."

"Honestly, it's good to be rid of him." She waved

her hand dismissively and started down the steps towards the parking lot.

"Mom." Kai sighed. "Could you at least try not to be insulting?"

"Kai, I get it, you're sad. But Ken was a terrible person, and I'm sure that whoever did this to him had a good reason." She paused, then looked into her son's eyes. "I'm sorry, I really am, Kai. I wish I'd chosen a better father for you."

"All right, enough Mom, let's just go get a car, okay?" His cheeks flushed as she nodded.

Suzie did her best to keep silent. She couldn't believe that someone would be so cruel to their own child. Couldn't Lisa see that Kai was in pain? If she did, she didn't seem to care.

As they drove through the town, Suzie pointed out a few restaurants that they might be interested in. Both Lisa and Kai remained silent. She pulled into the parking lot of Red's Rentals and parked near the front door.

"I'll walk you in. Red gives a discount to anyone that stays with us." She stepped out of the car and led them towards the door.

Lisa paused in front of it to read the advertise-ments on the door.

"Is this a trustworthy place?" She frowned. "I

know small businesses can be a little unreliable. I don't want a car that's going to give out on me."

"Look, Mom, they even put brand new tires on every car." Kai pointed to one of the signs on the door. "See, they have that special new tread that helps prevent hydroplaning. It's different to most tires. It's very wiggly." He pointed out the tread in the picture.

"Yes, I see." She glanced over at Suzie. "So? Reliable?"

"Yes, very. We've never had any trouble with cars that Red rents out, and neither have any of our guests." Suzie pulled the door open and held it for them both. Once on the other side she noticed just how much Lisa stood out in the small town surroundings.

"Great, because I don't want any more issues to come up. We just need to get this handled and get back home," Lisa said.

"I understand." Suzie walked up to the counter and introduced them to Red, then she turned to Lisa and Kai. "If you need anything, just let me or Mary know." She gave Lisa's shoulder a light pat, nodded to Kai, then headed back out the door.

CHAPTER 11

As Suzie settled back into her car, she knew exactly where she would go next. Her visit to town wasn't just for eggs. She parked outside of the medical examiner's office, then walked inside. She'd gotten to know Summer very well, especially since she and Jason were married. But she also knew that Summer was a professional, and it would probably be a bother to her to have her day interrupted. Still, she couldn't let the question in her mind rest any longer. She hoped that Summer would be able to shed some light on who the killer might be.

As she walked up to the front desk, the woman there offered her a light smile and nod.

"Suzie, I'm guessing you'd like to see Summer?"

"Yes, if she's not too busy."

"I'll just check." The receptionist left the room. A few moments later, Summer emerged from a swinging door down a short hallway. As the door swung open, Suzie heard music. She knew that Summer liked to listen to music while she worked.

"Suzie. I was wondering when I might get a visit from you." She smiled as she slipped her gloves off her hands, then tossed them in a nearby trashcan.

"Hi Summer, I'm sorry to bother you at work." Suzie lingered near the front desk.

"It's no problem." Summer smiled as she walked towards her. "What do you need?"

"I know you can't tell me specifically about Ken's murder, but I was wondering if you could tell me if someone with martial arts training could cause a fatal neck injury?"

"Sure, they could. But, so could anyone else. One wouldn't be able to tell the difference from the injury." Summer shook her head. "The victim's ability to defend themselves, like if they are intoxicated, the height of the perpetrator, all affects the type of injury."

"So really, anyone could cause that type of injury."

"Well no, they would have to be quite strong. Sorry, I can't tell you more than that."

"I know, thank you, Summer." She squeezed her hand, then released it. "I appreciate you giving me some time. It's hard not knowing if there might be a killer nearby."

"If you suspect anything, call Jason, he will make sure that you're safe." She smiled. "I have to get back to work."

"Thanks again, Summer."

~

Mary dug the spade into the window box and tried to adjust the soil around the freshly planted flowers. It gave her a sense of peace to work with plants, normally. Today however, it was frustrating. She'd tried to plant the flowers to brighten up the mood around the house, but from the start it was a difficult job. The plants didn't want to come out of their plastic containers. The soil was far too dry. The window box held less than she had anticipated. As she struggled with the placement of the flowers, she wondered if it had been wise to start such a task so close to dinner. She was just about to give up, when she heard voices drift towards her.

"All I'm saying is that you have to back off a

little bit." Sebastian's tone was stern, but hesitant at the same time.

"You're telling me what to do?" Bert's voice sounded incredulous.

"I'm not telling you what to do, Bert. I'm just suggesting that you be cautious and give Herb some room. The last thing we need is a big blow up while we're here, with all of this going on. I don't know what Callie or Herb will do if they found out."

"Herb wouldn't do anything. That's what Herb would do. He's all bark and no bite, you know that. You've seen that. What has you so worried, Seb?"

"I just think you're pushing things a little too far siding with Callie all the time, and you're keeping such a big secret. Have you even talked to Callie about any of it?"

"None of that is any of your business, Sebastian. I will let you know when I need your advice, understand?"

"Yes, sir. I'm sorry." Sebastian's voice lowered and softened in the same moment.

"I'd be more concerned about Tammy. I've seen the way you're throwing her around and you're getting too rough." It was Bert's turn to be stern.

"She doesn't complain. She says I don't hurt her."

"You may think you don't, but I've seen some bruising on her arms. Tammy is a tough woman, but when you cross a line and break something, you're going to have questions to answer, and the cops might not believe that she was okay with it. Got it? Not to mention, that you should not be losing control enough to be leaving marks on her body. If you're doing that, then you're not practicing the discipline techniques."

"Right, I know. You're right. I've been distracted. But, I don't often have anyone else to spar with."

"And no excuses. If I see a mark on her again, I'll show you some discipline myself, understand?"

"Yes sir, I'll be more careful."

"Good. And no more nonsense about Herb or Callie. As soon as this trip is over, things are going to change."

"All right, Bert." Sebastian cleared his throat, then Mary heard his footsteps approaching.

Would they know she had been listening? She dropped her spade and ducked behind some bushes before they walked past. She noticed that Bert hesitated for a moment at the bottom of the steps, then continued up onto the porch. Did he notice her there? She hoped not. It was odd that Sebastian had called him sir, and seemed so intimidated by him. But she was relieved that Bert had spoken to him about the way he handled Tammy. At least he wasn't afraid to speak up to his friend. But what was the issue between Herb, Bert, and Callie? And what secret was Bert keeping?

Curious, she decided to find out what she could about Bert. She dialed Wes' number and hoped that he might have a few minutes to spare. Luckily, he answered quickly.

"Mary, how are you?"

"I'm doing okay. I know you're busy, but if you have a few minutes, I've become very curious about Bert, the leader of the birdwatching group."

"Bert?" He paused. "Why are you curious about him?"

"I just overheard snippets of a conversation that made me a bit suspicious, and I'm getting an odd vibe from him. I thought maybe you could look into him, see if he's had any criminal issues in the past, or anything else that you might consider unusual."

"Sure, I can do that. I'll let you know what I come up with. But, are you sure you're telling me everything?"

"Yes, I am. It's just really a gut instinct, nothing more than that."

"Okay, I'll let you know as soon as I find something. Have a good day, Mary."

"Thanks, you too." She hung up the phone, then released a long breath. She wondered if he'd find anything, or if she was just being paranoid. Either way, she knew that someone, likely someone under her roof, knew something about Ken's death. It crossed her mind that Lisa could have had something to do with it, as hateful as she was about Ken. But she was not even in the state when his death occurred, and the death didn't strike her as a professional hit. But then maybe it was made to look that way to avoid suspicion.

When she saw Jason's patrol car pull into the parking lot, she headed out to meet him. He stepped out of the car and pulled off his hat as she approached.

"Hi Mary. Is Suzie here, too?"

"No, she went into town." She searched his eyes. "Did something happen?"

"Not exactly. I just wanted to take another look around the house, maybe speak to some of the guests again."

"They were pretty riled up last time." Mary frowned.

"I understand, and I'm sorry about that. But,

I've eliminated just about all the surfers, including Noel, as suspects, which leaves me with your group, and I was told Kai is staying here as well?"

"Yes, he is, but he's in town with his mother, as far as I know. How did you eliminate Noel?"

"He has an alibi." He leaned back against the car and pulled out his notepad. "I've confirmed it. There's no way he committed the crime. Most of the other surfers were with him at the time, and they have videos of them singing around the fire. I've identified everyone in the video around the time of death, and the only one of their group that wasn't there was Kai."

"Where does he say he was?" Mary narrowed her eyes.

"He claims he went for a walk on the beach. He was embarrassed by his father's argument with Noel, and decided to blow off some steam. He's not on the video, and no one can place exactly what time he left or came back. But according to both Kai and Noel, Ken walked into those woods. Which leads me to believe that maybe it was someone who saw him go into the woods, or ran into him in the woods. There aren't any other houses around. None of the nearby parking lot cameras show video of anyone parking near the woods or the beach, but they don't cover the whole area. My best guess is that it was someone on foot, someone close enough to walk into the woods, and walk back out, without drawing any attention."

"I see." She shivered a little as she considered the possibilities. For a moment, she thought about sharing her suspicions about both Bert and Sebastian, but since she had nothing solid to share, she decided against it. "Well, of course you can go right in and speak to them, but be careful, Jason. Herb is very annoyed, and Sebastian is much, much, stronger than he looks."

"I will be." He placed his hand on her shoulder and looked into her eyes. "You've got nothing to worry about, Mary, I'm going to get to the bottom of this, I promise."

"Thanks, Jason." She watched as he walked up to the house. She knew that he'd only asked her out of courtesy, he had every right to speak to the guests, but he did his best not to step on her or Suzie's toes when possible.

She sent a text to Suzie to update her on the latest development. Noel had been in her sights as a suspect, but now that he'd been eliminated, it only left them a few people to consider. Kai, of course, as much as she hated to admit it. Sebastian, with his temper and martial arts skills. And now, as he stuck in her mind, Bert, who she now believed was hiding something. She couldn't rule out Herb either, even though Callie claimed to be with him the entire night. She might have given her husband a fake alibi or maybe she didn't know if he snuck out. As she tapped out the message on her phone, she hoped that Jason was right, and all of this would be wrapped up soon.

CHAPTER 12

*A*fter leaving the medical examiner's office, Suzie headed for the library. She wanted to see what she could find out about the type of injury that Ken suffered, and also return a few books that were due. When she stepped in she waved to Louis, the librarian, who was stationed at his usual perch behind his large desk. He waved back, then turned back to the book in his hand. He wasn't the friendliest librarian, but when she needed information he was always willing to give it. However, before she could walk over to the desk, her cell phone chimed with a text.

Louis glanced up with a furrowed brow and pursed lips. She blushed as she switched the phone to silent. Then she saw the text was from Mary. She read it over, and felt her heart fall. She'd been convinced that Noel was the killer. Now it was clear that he wasn't. Or at least, it seemed to be clear. The suspicion still nagged at the back of her mind. As she approached the desk again, Louis watched her with curiosity.

"What are you up to today?"

"I just need to drop these off and use one of the computers." She handed over the library books. "I want to do a quick search, and I hate typing detailed information on my phone."

"Sure, go ahead." He tipped his head back towards the rows of computers. "Or do you need a private one?"

"No, that should be fine. Thanks, Louis." As she walked towards the computers, she noticed that one was occupied by someone familiar.

"Noel, I didn't expect to see you here." She offered him a small smile.

"Yes, I surf and read." He smiled in return as he spun towards her in the computer chair. "I'm here to get a little local information, about your house actually."

"My house?" She raised an eyebrow. "Well, anything you might want to know about it, you can always ask me."

"I've heard around town that you inherited it

from your uncle, but I suspect it was part of an old movie I've seen. It looks just like it. I haven't been able to shake the thought. But no matter how much searching I do, I can't seem to find a connection. Are you familiar with 'In the Surf'?"

"No, I've never heard of it." She frowned. "I would think someone would have told me if it was in a movie. I've never heard anything about it."

"Ah well, maybe it's my imagination. You should check out the movie sometime and see what you think. Then give me a call if you agree." He handed her his business card. "We'll only be here a few more days, but you can contact me anytime."

"Thanks, I will let you know." She tucked the card into her purse. "I know it must be tough for you to keep the trip going after losing Ken. It must be even harder for you, since you had a few run-ins with him."

"At least the police have finally stopped questioning me about it." He shook his head. "I'm telling you they were ready to slap the cuffs on me and lock me away. But I have an alibi, I was with other campers all night. It's been verified over and over. I have the all clear, and now that the approximate time of death has been determined, the other campers know I had nothing to do with it, but it's still hard to get them focused on relaxing and surfing again."

"I imagine it must be. I'll let you know if I find out anything more about the house."

"Thanks." He nodded to her before he walked out of the library.

She turned back to look at Louis. "Was that really what he was looking for?"

"Yes, I told him he should just ask you, but apparently you don't know anything more than I do." Louis gazed at her as his glasses slid down his nose. "Shocking."

"Sorry, I've never heard of any movie being filmed at the house. It makes me wonder whether that was what he was really looking for."

"Didn't he say he was cleared by the police?" Louis looked towards the door. "Are you still thinking he might be involved?"

"I'm thinking that someone killed Ken, and even though Noel has an alibi, I still think he might be hiding something." She sighed as she met Louis' eyes. "Do you think I'm just being paranoid?"

"I don't know how you couldn't be, Suzie. What happened just down the beach from your home, your business, it's enough to make anyone paranoid. But everyone can't be the murderer." He tapped his fingertip on the desk. "Only one person killed Ken, I would guess, and it was a rushed experience with no real time to cover up the crime. I don't think anyone planned it."

"What gives you that perspective?"

"I've been reading a lot of murder mysteries, lately." He smiled. "I'd rather read about them than live them."

"Me too." Suzie sighed, then settled at the computer that Noel had just been using. As she started to type her query into the search bar, the entire question popped up after she only entered a few letters, as if someone had recently searched the same thing. Her stomach twisted as she stared at the text. That had nothing to do with a movie, or Dune House. Someone had looked up information about fatal neck injuries, and she doubted that was a common thing to do. Nervously, she looked back at Louis, who already had his nose buried back in his book. Was it possible that Noel had somehow faked his alibi?

According to Mary's text there was video of him around the campfire at the time of Ken's death. How could he be in two places at once? She knew it was impossible, and Jason would have made certain that the video hadn't been altered. But someone had searched the information on the computer, and recently. She stood up and walked over to Louis' desk.

"Have any of the birdwatchers been in the library recently?"

"You'll have to be more specific, unless they all wear some special kind of hat." Louis chuckled.

"Let's see, Herb and Callie, they're about ten years younger than me. Then there's Sebastian and Tammy, they're in their thirties. And lastly there is Bert, he's quite a few years older than me. Have you met any of them?" She showed him a group picture of them she'd taken on their birdwatching excursion.

"Sebastian and Tammy were in here, and Bert, too. He wanted to know if there were any local pet shops that specialized in exotic pets. Sebastian and Tammy spent most of their time in the physical fitness section."

"Did any of them use the computer?"

"Yes, all three of them, actually. Sorry, but I don't think I'd be able to sort out their internet activity at this point, we've had a lot of people using the computers today, and yesterday."

"That's all right." She frowned. "Thanks for the information, Louis."

"Anytime, Suzie." He turned back to his book.

As she left the library, an eerie feeling passed through her. Was it possible that one of them had just been curious, like she was, about how Ken was killed and decided to look up the injury? She knew that it was, but it still seemed strange. Maybe she was being paranoid.

~

*M*ary received a text back from Suzie that she was on her way, and had picked up the eggs. She smiled to herself, impressed that she'd remembered. A few seconds later her phone rang.

"Hi Suzie." She laughed. "Did you forget the eggs after all?"

"It's me, Wes. Do you need eggs?"

"Oh sorry, Wes, I didn't look at the phone before I answered." Mary laughed. "No, Suzie is picking some up."

"It's all right. Are you there alone?"

"The guests are upstairs. Why?" Her heartbeat quickened at the concern in his voice.

"I looked into Bert, like you asked. He doesn't have any criminal record, but there are some

CINDY BELL

unusual patterns in his life. He can't seem to keep a business partner, or a spouse. He was married about forty years ago for a very brief time, but since then I can't see any indication of a relationship. There's nothing criminal about that, but it can be a warning sign of a personality problem. Have you noticed anything strange about the way he interacts with the others?"

"He seems fairly laid back." She bit into her bottom lip. "He does seem a little dominant around Sebastian, it struck me as odd."

"Just be cautious around him. There's nothing in his past that would indicate he's violent. I can come over this evening if you would like."

"I'd like that very much. If you're not too busy of course."

"I'll make sure I'm not. See you tonight."

After he hung up the phone she mulled over his words. It was good news that Bert didn't have a criminal past, but the caution in Wes' voice made her uneasy. She was relieved when she saw Suzie's car pull into the parking lot. She headed to the door to greet her.

"Mary, I've got some interesting information." She handed the eggs over to her. "And the eggs."

"Great, I need these for the quiche I'm making for dinner. Can we talk while I cook?"

"Sure." Suzie followed her into the kitchen.

As she filled her in on what she found at the library, Mary shared what Wes had told her about Bert.

"That's interesting," Suzie nodded. "But it might mean nothing."

"I agree." Mary smiled, but she couldn't shake her suspicion of him.

Once dinner was in the oven, she and Suzie set the table. Mary wondered if anyone would even show up for dinner. To her surprise, when she took the quiche out of the oven, everyone was already seated around the table. She noticed that no one seemed to be talking to each other, however. Suzie helped her get all of the food onto the table, then they settled into their chairs.

"It's a little quiet in here." Suzie raised an eyebrow. "Is everything okay?"

"The police paid another visit today." Herb rolled his eyes. "I thought they were supposed to serve and protect, not harass."

"He's just trying to do his job, Herb." Callie frowned. "If you were a little bit more patient."

"Patient with a man who is trying to accuse me

of murder? Are you kidding me?" He stood up from the table without eating a bite of his food. "That's it, we're going out to dinner. I need a break from all of this." Herb grabbed her hand.

"Okay. Let's go find somewhere to eat." Callie stood up.

"Are you sure about this, Callie?" Bert stared at the couple.

"Yes, it's fine."

"See? What we do is none of your business." Herb glared across the table at Bert. "It's fine. Now back off." He led Callie away from the table and out the door.

Mary felt some relief to see them go. She didn't like that Callie had to deal with Herb's attitude, but she also preferred not to have to deal with it at the dinner table.

"I don't know why she puts up with him." Tammy shook her head. "If you ever even thought of treating me that way, Sebastian."

"I would never." He took her hand and kissed the back of it. "You're my treasure, you know that, Tammy."

Mary's heart softened at the display.

"Let's try to enjoy our meal." Suzie smiled. She was touched by Sebastian's interaction with Tammy.

Perhaps, she was wrong to judge him so harshly when she saw the way he sparred with her.

"Yes, let's." Bert nodded to Suzie and Mary. "It was kind of you to prepare this for us. I know that you both have a lot on your minds, too."

"It was no trouble." Mary smiled as she studied Bert. "We like to try to create a homey feel, that's why we provide home-style meals. Is that something you enjoy, Bert?"

"I suppose it is, I'm enjoying it right now." He chuckled. "It sure beats the bachelor pad back home."

"I'm glad." She smiled. "You're such a lovely man I'm sure that you'll find someone to come home to soon."

"Mary, are you flirting with me?" He grinned.

"Excuse me?" Wes stood in the doorway, several feet away from the dining room, but close enough to hear Bert's words.

"No, of course not." Her cheeks flamed red.

Suzie took an extra sip of her wine, then set her glass down.

"Wes, let me grab you a plate. Mary, will you help me?" She stood up and walked around the table to pat her friend on the shoulder.

"It's all right if you were, Mary, but I don't feel

there's much of a connection between us." Bert shrugged.

"There isn't." Wes pulled out a chair and sat down at the table. He locked eyes with Bert as he did. "She was just being kind. She's a very kind person."

"So, I see." Bert tipped his head to the side. "Do I detect some jealousy in your tone?"

"Bert, leave it alone." Sebastian frowned. "It was just a misunderstanding."

"I'm sure it was." Wes thrust his hand across the table. "I'm Wes, Mary's boyfriend."

"Boyfriend?" Mary mouthed the word to Suzie as the two pretended to need two people to make up one plate of food.

"Well, what else would you call him?" Suzie shooed her away from the plate. "Go back out there before things get more tense."

"What if Wes really thinks I was flirting with Bert?" Mary sighed. "What if I hurt his feelings?"

"Wes is a smart man, he knows he can trust you, Mary."

"I hope so." She clasped her hands together as she headed back to the table. "Wes, I'm so glad you could join us."

"Me, too." He smiled up at her.

The rest of dinner went smoothly. Despite Mary's initial concern, Wes didn't seem to be upset by Bert's comment. Still, she looked forward to giving him a clearer explanation when they had some time alone. However, just as she was clearing the dinner dishes, Wes' phone rang.

"I'm sorry, Mary, I have to run, it's about a case." He pulled her in for a quick kiss. "I'll be back tonight, as soon as I can."

"That's fine, I understand." She gave his hand a squeeze. "Don't worry about me."

"I always will." He kissed the back of her hand, then headed for the door.

Mary watched him go, and wondered just what he might be thinking about Bert. Was there more to his visit than just to check on her?

CHAPTER 13

*A*s they cleaned up from dinner, Suzie stole a few glances at Mary. She thought her friend was acting a little strange. She had a faraway look in her eyes and every time Suzie attempted to start a conversation she didn't engage in it.

"How about I make us some tea to take outside?" Suzie pulled two mugs down from the cabinet.

"That sounds perfect." Mary nodded. She grabbed some teabags from the cabinet beside her.

"Mary, you know that Wes didn't take Bert seriously, right?" She waited for the kettle to whistle.

"I know." She sighed. "At least I think I do." She looked over at Suzie. "Am I supposed to be this concerned at my age? I just feel like Wes and I are still getting to know each other in a lot of ways, and I'm not sure if he totally trusts me."

"Age has nothing to do with it. Yes, things between you and Wes are still blossoming. But he knows you well enough to know that you wouldn't do anything to hurt him." She poured the hot water over the tea bags while Mary grabbed some sugar packets.

"I hope so." Mary picked up the mugs as they walked out onto the porch. She noticed Pilot resting in the yard that had been fenced-off for him. The beach was quiet.

"I haven't seen Kai and Lisa. I hope they're finding everything they need okay."

"Are they settled into their rooms?" Suzie sat down next to Mary and smiled as she accepted the mug of tea from her. They sat close so they could speak softly without others overhearing. "Ah, this is just what I needed. Some hot tea, and quality Mary time."

"Yes, I think we could both use some time to unwind tonight. What a crazy day it's been." She closed her eyes for a moment, then nodded. "Yes, I think they're settled in. Neither came down to dinner, but I'm pretty sure they were up in their rooms. Callie and Herb haven't come back yet." She took a sip of her tea, then set the cup down. "Suzie, something just feels so off, doesn't it? I can't seem to settle down."

"I understand what you mean. I keep looking over my shoulder, too. My instincts are telling me that danger is closer to home than we realize." She pursed her lips as she looked towards the windows that faced the porch. "Maybe having Kai and his mother stay here was a mistake."

"I don't think so, Suzie. It's the only way we can try and keep him safe."

"And if he killed his father?" She set her tea down and looked across the table at her friend. "We both know that's a possibility."

"Yes." She nodded. "I do know that. If he is the killer, at least we'll be able to keep a close eye on him."

"That's true. And it's not likely that if he is the killer, he'll want to do anything to hurt anyone else. If the argument was between himself and his father, then clearly it has ended, and no one else should be in danger. Still, it makes me nervous to think it's a possibility."

"Honestly, I'm more concerned about someone else in this house." Mary frowned as she recalled Wes' suspicions about Bert.

"Who? Sebastian?" Suzie sat forward in her chair and studied Mary's expression.

"Bert." She looked towards the windows then back to Suzie. "I know what Wes found out about him doesn't mean much, but I do want to find out more about him." She shook her head. "I guess I really suspect everyone to a degree. Don't you?"

"Absolutely. We can't be sure of the killer's motive, and that means we can't be sure that he won't attack again. I want you to be careful."

"I'll be as careful as you are." She smiled. "I promise."

"Nice." Suzie laughed, then shook her head. "Well, I plan on being very careful, so keep that in mind."

"I will do my best." She squeezed Suzie's hand. "Thank you, for always looking out for me."

"I always will, Mary, I promise." Suzie gazed into her eyes for a long moment.

"The same goes for you, Suzie." She caught sight of a figure moving along the beach out of the corner of her eye. There was Sebastian, alone. A moment later, she saw Bert join him. The two seemed to be in a heated discussion, then Sebastian followed Bert along the beach in the opposite direction of the woods. "I wonder what those two are up to?"

"I know what I'm going to be up to. Paul should be here any minute." She smiled. "I can't wait to see him."

"When is his next trip out?"

"Too soon." She frowned. "You know it used to be that I really enjoyed him leaving for a few days at a time, it gave us the chance to look forward to seeing each other. But these last few trips have seemed very long, I have to admit."

"Aw, that's sweet." Mary leaned close, her eyes shone. "Someone's in love."

"Enough of that!" Suzie waved her hand and laughed.

"Mmhm." Mary finished her tea.

A knock on the door drew Suzie's attention. "That must be Paul now. We're back here, Paul!"

"You two have a good night together. Try not to think about the case, all right? I'll make myself scarce so that you can have some time together."

"You don't have to do that, Mary. I think we're just going to talk about the murder, anyway." Suzie started towards the door.

"You shouldn't. Just spend some time together, Suzie. Paul just got back from his trip, have you even had a chance to really talk to him?" She headed inside and straight for the stairs.

"No, I guess I haven't." She smiled as she saw Paul round the front porch and head in their direction.

"Then do." Mary rested her hand on her friend's shoulder. "Savor the time you have, that's one lesson I've learned."

"I'll do my best. Goodnight, Mary."

"Goodnight, Suzie, see you in the morning." She stepped inside the house, sparing a brief glance over her shoulder in Suzie's direction. She hoped that she and Paul would decide to head out for the night, because she didn't want to get them involved in what she was about to do. She didn't want to ruin their night.

Suzie stared after her for a moment. It wasn't often that Mary would go to bed so early. She would usually have at least a brief conversation with Paul. She suspected that her friend was up to something, but she decided not to question it. Too often she treated Mary as if she couldn't handle herself, when she absolutely could.

Paul walked up to the table, his gaze focused on Mary's retreating form.

"Headed to bed?"

"Yes, I think she wanted us to have some alone

time." She slipped her hand into his. "I'm just glad you're here."

"Me too." He wrapped her up in a tight hug, then took a deep breath. "Honestly, it's good just to be with you. It was a long jaunt at sea this time, with all of the stress of the repairs, and then Ken's death, I feel like I've hardly had the chance to spend time with you."

"Trust me, I'd love nothing more than to just take a walk with you." She met his eyes.

"I see where this is going." He smiled some. "It wouldn't be a romantic walk would it?"

"I just want to take another look at the place where Ken died. I feel like I'm missing something. There has to be some kind of clue to what happened there. What still sticks out in my mind are those broken branches. Someone was in that tree, and I have no idea why. I thought we might come across something if we just took another stroll. Jason texted me a little while ago to let me know they opened the trail back up. I know that Bert has been itching to get back out there, so if we have any chance of finding anything it has to be now, before it gets trampled."

"All right, I understand. It does make sense to go out there. But if we're going to go, we should do it now, before it gets too much later." He slipped his hand into hers.

"Yes, let's go, I want to know who did this, and if there's some clue there that the police overlooked, I want the chance to find it."

"We need to be as quiet as we can. If anyone's keeping an eye on the woods, then we're going to get the wrong kind of attention." Paul tightened his grasp on her hand.

Suzie nodded, as her heart skipped a beat. They started out across the sand. The rush of the waves attempted to soothe her, but she couldn't let go of her anxiety. What if she didn't find anything in the woods? What if there really was no way to prove who killed Ken?

"Paul, who do you think did this? You haven't really said."

"My money is on Kai. I know that Mary has a soft spot for him. But I know what it's like to have a problem with your father." He glanced at her as they neared the woods. "My father and I went our rounds, and no I wouldn't have killed him, but I did wish him dead a time or two."

"You did?" She stared at him with wide eyes. "Why?"

"Because I was a teenager, and I was sure I

knew everything there was to know. Because, he wasn't the man I thought he should be." He shrugged. "There's no good reason really. Nothing that makes sense now that he's gone. I still feel guilty about it at times, and I am so grateful that it never got to the point that I said things I would spend the rest of my life regretting. Kai got pushed to his limit by his father, I think it's possible that it was enough for him to lose it."

"I guess I can understand that, but he still seems like such a sweet kid. His mom, she's a far different story. I'd be certain that she did it, if she wasn't out of state when it happened."

"Maybe she was out of state, but Kai was here. If she had that much animosity towards Ken, that might have played a part in his actions. Maybe he thought he was defending his mother. Whatever the case, I can't think of anyone else having a reason to kill Ken. Can you?" He paused at the start of the trail.

"Maybe. I could have sworn it was Noel. I'm still not convinced that he didn't play a part in it." She put her finger to her lips as she started down the trail. If someone was nearby she didn't want to alert them to their presence. They even kept their flashlights turned off, which made the woods seem thicker and darker. Suzie shivered as she continued further along the trail. Even though she'd walked it many times at night, this night it felt far different. She couldn't shake the feeling that someone else was there in the woods with them.

CHAPTER 14

Mary looked out the window one more time to make sure that Bert wasn't heading back towards the house. Then she slid the key into the lock. She crept into the room, she wasn't sure why? She had the perfect excuse if she was caught, she just wanted to drop off the towels she had forgotten to replenish, but a sense of danger ran through her. What if he really was keeping some big secret and he was worried she had found it out? What if he returned unexpectedly? She might only have minutes to investigate, but she knew it could be her only chance to see if her hunch was right, and he was the one who killed Ken. Then the risk was worth it.

As she started walking past the bedside table

something on it immediately caught her attention. There was a small notebook. It was lying open on the table, and on closer inspection she could see that the cover was worn. Without touching it she looked at the page it was open to. It was on the page dated that morning. She presumed it was the most recent entry. From the layout of the entry and the size of the book she guessed that it was a private diary, something he'd had for quite some time. Would he really confess to murder in a diary? She had no idea, but she was going to find out. She read over the words, and her mind began to spin. Her heartbeat quickened as she picked up the book and began flipping back through the pages to see if there was more information to find. She sat down on the edge of the bed as she realized there were pages and pages filled with the same thoughts, feelings and revelations, that she had never sensed from him. Her stomach twisted as her hunch grew even stronger. Maybe anger wasn't much of a motive, not enough for Bert to stalk and kill Ken, but love and family might just be.

Through the open bedroom window, she heard voices. Her mind spun. Was it Bert? Had he returned already? She put the book back the same way she had found it. It wasn't enough to prove that

Bert had killed Ken, but if it was the big secret that Sebastian referred to it might be enough to drive Bert away if the truth got out. For now, she needed to keep it to herself. She realized, it was Suzie and Paul's voices just below her on the porch. She listened closely and was able to catch the tail end of their conversation. She knew that they were headed out to the woods. But what if that was where Bert went?

Suzie and Paul might be walking into something they didn't expect. She slipped out of Bert's room, hoping that she had left everything exactly how it had been. If he noticed that someone had looked through his things, she imagined that he would be quite angry. As she reached the first floor, she decided to take Pilot with her, just in case. He could serve as protection and he was also a very good detective. He could sniff out details that she might overlook.

"Pilot, here boy! Come here, pups." She called for him. When the dog didn't respond she looked through the window to check the yard. Pilot wasn't there so she assumed that he must have gone with Suzie and Paul. She headed out the door to catch up with them. She kicked herself for not telling Suzie her plans earlier. But Bert seemed like such a nice man, even after she discovered what secret he was keeping. There was no mention of Ken's murder. Just because he was keeping a secret that didn't make him a murderer. Maybe Bert ran into Ken in the woods again and they got into an argument. Then the argument had taken an ugly turn and Bert had reacted. But that didn't change the fact that Bert was much older than Ken. Ken was a strong, young man when compared to Bert. How could Bert have overpowered him? She hurried across the beach, eager to catch up with Paul and Suzie. Maybe they could help her figure all of this out.

Before she could get to the woods, she noticed a lone figure on the beach. She was certain he had noticed her, too. Bert stared at her as the moonlight shone down on him. There was no mistaking who it was. Too shocked to move, she waited for him to approach her. Instead, he turned, and began to walk towards the woods, the same woods that Suzie and Paul had been heading towards. Her heart dropped in the same moment that her feet started moving in the direction he went. If he got to Suzie and Paul before she did, there might be a bigger problem to deal with. Why had he stared at her that way? He hadn't waved, hadn't nodded, he'd just stared. It left her unsettled, and once more suspicious of his intentions.

❧

Suzie bent down to look at a broken twig, then suddenly froze with fear. Her eyes were on a pair of shoes, only a few feet away from her. The shock of it kept her silent, until her mind finally made the connection that the shoes belonged to Mary. She looked up at her and took a sharp breath.

"What are you doing out here, Mary? You startled me."

"I'm sorry, I wanted to check on you and Paul." She glanced around the surrounding woods. "I thought someone might be following you. Did you see anyone out here?"

"No, and unfortunately, I'm not seeing much evidence that points to a killer, either. I've looked all throughout this area, and whatever the killer might have left behind must have been swept away by the forensics team."

"Mary?" Paul walked over to them. "I didn't know you planned to join us."

"I didn't plan it." She frowned. "Listen, Suzie, I found something."

"Really, what?" Suzie gazed eagerly into her eyes.

"Wait, there's someone else here." Paul placed his hand on Suzie's shoulder and put his finger to his lips.

Suzie swiveled her gaze from one end of the woods to the other. Like Paul, she could sense another presence, but she couldn't see one. After a moment Paul shook his head.

"I'm sorry, I must be letting my imagination get carried away."

"Mary, what were you going to say?" Suzie turned back to look at her, and found an empty space where she had once stood. "Where did she go? Where's Mary?" Suzie's heart slammed against her chest. "She was just right here. Paul, did you see where she went?"

"No, I didn't." He frowned, then shined his flashlight through the trees. "Maybe she wandered off?"

"Mary!" Suzie shouted her name so loudly that it hurt her ears and strained her throat.

"Sh! Suzie!" Paul wrapped his arms around her. "What happened to being quiet?"

"I'm not going to be quiet. Mary's gone, Paul! She's not answering me! Someone must have taken her!" She could hardly get her words out as she gasped for air. Her lungs felt so tight that she wasn't sure she'd be able to ever breathe fully again. She could recall moments before having Mary's hand in hers. How could she just disappear?

"All right, she has to be here somewhere." Paul shone his flashlight through the trees again, and this time his brows were knitted with concern. "Mary!" He shouted, even louder than Suzie had.

Again, there was no response.

"Paul! Where is she?" Suzie began to run through the woods. She ignored Paul's pleas for her to return to the trail. As she ran, she pulled out her phone and dialed Mary's number. When she heard her ringtone, a sense of relief washed over her. Until she spotted the phone hidden under some brush. "Oh no, oh no." She grabbed the phone, and turned to face Paul who had run up behind her. "Paul, someone took her. She's gone!"

"We need to call Jason." He pulled out his phone. "He can get the floodlights up here. Maybe she just got turned around and dropped her phone."

Within minutes another figure began jogging up the trail.

"Jason?" Suzie shined her flashlight at the figure, and discovered it was Wes. "Wes! Have you seen Mary?"

"Seen her? No. I'm here looking for her. Isn't she with you?" He removed his hat as he looked around.

"No, I think she's been taken, Wes. She was here one second, then gone the next."

"What do you mean she's been taken?" He looked between both of them. "Weren't you here with her? How could you not see who took her?"

"I don't know." Suzie's eyes filled with tears. "One moment she was there and the next she was gone. It was dark, and then I found her cell phone. I think the killer took her, but I have no idea why."

"She must have been on to something." Wes winced and pressed his hand against his forehead. "She said she suspected Bert. She wanted to know more about him. She asked me to look him up. But I didn't find anything solid that would point to him as the killer. Did Mary come out here with you?"

"No." Paul looked back at the trail. "She caught up with us, but then a few minutes later she disappeared."

"Did she say anything to you? Did she mention

anything." Wes gazed into Suzie's eyes, his own widened desperately.

"We'd been talking about Kai, and also Noel, and all of the guests really. But we hadn't settled on any of them. We both said it didn't feel quite right." Her stomach twisted as she tried to remember Mary's exact words. It was difficult for her to pin anything down when they had so many conversations about all of the suspects. "Wait. All we need to do is see who is missing, right? If it was someone we suspected, and if that person still has Mary, then we probably won't be able to find them."

"Well, even if we see someone, that doesn't mean that they don't have her. They could have stashed her somewhere and then come out into public so they wouldn't look guilty." Paul shoved his hands in his pockets. "I don't think that's going to tell us anything."

Before Wes could reply his phone chimed with a text.

"It's Jason." Wes looked at his phone. "He's going to send a search party through the woods, but I don't think they're going to find her out there."

"You're right." Suzie groaned. "I can't just stand here, I have to find her. Pilot! We need Pilot! If anyone can find her, he can." She ran back towards the house. As she approached she saw the flashing lights in the parking lot for the beach. She knew that Jason would do everything he could to find Mary, but where would he begin to look. That was the problem. Mary vanished, and she could be anywhere. Hopefully, Pilot would be able to pick up Mary's scent and lead Suzie straight to Mary. But he wasn't outside and when she entered the house and called for him, there was no response. She called several more times, then realized that the dog was not in the house. He was missing, again.

She turned just as Paul stepped through the door.

"Pilot's not here." She fought back another flood of tears. "He's missing, too. Now, how am I going to find her, Paul?"

"It's all right, Suzie, we're going to find her." He hugged her. "Should we call her kids? Let them know what's happened?"

"No, not yet. Mary wouldn't want them to worry." She looked up as Wes stepped through the door. "Pilot's not here."

"Okay, I'm going to check with the guests upstairs. See if any of them have seen Mary or Pilot." Wes grimaced.

"We'll help." Suzie started towards the stairs. As

they reached the top of the stairs they spread out. Suzie went straight to Mary's room, hoping that maybe somehow she had returned to the house. She knocked, then when there was no answer used her key. Her heart fell when she saw that Mary wasn't in the room. She walked back to find Wes and Paul.

"No one is answering." Wes frowned. "Can you unlock the doors so we can check if anyone is in there?"

"Of course." Suzie nodded. As they started to go from room to room Wes' cell rang. He moved to the end of the hallway as he answered the phone. Paul and Suzie continued to go from room to room to check if anyone was there. But no one was in their rooms. "This is so strange." Suzie's heartbeat quickened. "I thought that only Herb and Callie might still be out."

Wes walked quickly back towards them with his cell phone in his hand.

"I think we might have a lead. Someone in the search party found tire tracks on the other side of the woods. My guess is someone grabbed her from the woods and put her in a vehicle to get her away as quick as possible. He sent a picture." He displayed the photograph to Suzie. She stared at it for a long moment, then gasped.

"It was Lisa's car! I know those tires. I've seen the same pattern at the rental place in town. I took Kai and his mother there, so they could rent a car. They all have this style tire, it's something they advertise."

"Let's go out there and have a look." Wes lead the way down the stairs.

CHAPTER 15

*P*aul drove Suzie and Wes to the edge of the woods, where they met the road. Police officers were already there, with the scene roped off.

"We're not going to be able to get too close." Paul shook his head.

"Don't worry, I can get us a look." Wes stepped out of the car, flashed his badge, then escorted them to the section of dirt that was surrounded by cones. Suzie nodded as she looked over the tire marks.

"That's the same tread, I'm sure of it."

Wes peered at the tire tracks in the dirt. "Someone put her in this vehicle. I'm sure that Jason is tracking down the owner of the rental place right now to see who rented cars from there. But you said Kai's mother rented one. I think it's pretty safe to assume that they are the ones who took her. We should start with them. What can you tell me about them?"

"Not much, actually." Suzie stared at him, her eyes wide. "We usually take copies of identification when we book someone, but since we let them stay for free, and considering the circumstances, I didn't even think about it to be honest."

"All right, well firstly we need to know if they're driving the vehicle that matches these tire tracks. Do you think you could get Kai to the house if you called him?" He looked into Suzie's eyes as they headed back to the woods.

"I can try." She dialed Kai's number as they pulled up at the house. The young man picked up on the second ring.

"Hi Suzie, what's up?"

"Kai, I need you to come back to the house, please." She did her best to keep her voice calm. She didn't want to tip him off that they were on to him.

"I am at the house."

"You are?" She paused as she neared the porch. Then she heard a familiar bark. Pilot bounded around the corner towards her.

Paul and Wes watched as Suzie greeted the dog, then the man that followed after him.

"I was looking everywhere for him. What were you doing with him?" She eyed him.

"He looked like he needed a walk." Kai frowned as the dog licked Suzie's hand. "I didn't think that you would mind."

"I do mind." Suzie grabbed Pilot's collar and held it tight. "Where is Mary, Kai?"

"What? I don't know. Why?" He shoved his hands in his pockets. "I didn't mean to upset you."

"You were out in the woods tonight, weren't you? Why would you take her?" Suzie glared at him. "You tell me where she is!"

"Suzie! Stop!" Kai took a few steps back. "I have no idea what you're talking about. I took Pilot out on the beach. We didn't go anywhere near the woods. Pilot wanted to, but I wouldn't let him, I couldn't stand the thought of seeing where my father died. I would never do anything to hurt Mary. She's been so kind to me through all of this, you both have been."

"Did you see anyone else while you were out on the beach?" Paul stepped forward.

Suzie continued to watch Kai, not convinced that he was telling the truth. Mary was certain he had nothing to do with his father's death, but she had never explained why, beyond intuition. Had

CINDY BELL

he betrayed that feeling by abducting her, or worse?

"Yes, I saw Bert." He glanced towards the woods. "I saw him go up the trail into the woods. I figured he was out looking for that bird again. Wait, what happened to Mary? Is she okay?" His tone grew anxious.

"You tell us." Wes locked eyes with Kai. "I'm not playing games here, son, I want to know where she is."

"I don't know what you think I did, but I had nothing to do with it. I'm not going to listen to this." He turned and started to walk away.

"Wait, Kai, where's your mother? Where's the car that she rented?" Suzie released Pilot's collar, but the dog remained right by her side.

"My mom spent the night at my lawyer's house. I know how that sounds." His cheeks flushed. "As far as I know he picked her up. The car should be in the parking lot."

"I'll check for it!" Wes jogged towards the parking lot. Suzie started to follow after him, but Kai caught her by the arm.

"Suzie, wait. I wouldn't do anything to Mary, you have to believe me. If there's anything that I can do to help, I'll do it." He looked into her eyes.

"I'm sorry for accusing you, Kai. Do you know the address of the lawyer your mother hired? I want to make sure that she's safe." She felt a little relief as he released her arm. As much as she wanted to believe him, she had no idea what happened to Mary, and until she was back home, everyone was a suspect to her.

"Sure, I've got it here." He pulled out his wallet and handed her a business card. "His home and office address are on here."

"Thank you." She took the business card, snapped a picture, and texted it along with the information Kai shared, to Jason.

"Kai, why don't you come into the house with us." Paul tipped his head towards the house. "We're not sure what's happening here, but it'll be better if everyone is together."

"What about Bert?" Kai glanced over his shoulder. "Didn't you see him in the woods?"

"No, I didn't see him." Paul looked over at Suzie. "Let's go, sweetheart, there's nothing more we can do out here."

"I'll be there in just a moment." She watched as they walked towards the front door. Paul looked back in her direction, and she knew he was hesitant to leave her behind, but she was determined to take one more look through the woods, now that she had Pilot at her side.

Leaves crunched under her feet as Pilot led her up the trail.

"Where is she, pups? Can you find her? Where's Mary?" Just speaking those words made her chest ache with fear. She should know exactly where Mary was. She should have been safe at home, instead of out wandering the woods alone. Maybe, if Suzie hadn't gone out into the woods in the first place, Mary wouldn't have been taken.

Pilot's insistent barking broke through the spiral of guilt that threatened to overtake her. She watched as the dog rushed towards a thin trail, where some branches and brush had been broken. She followed after Pilot, expecting him to run towards the road, where the tire tracks had been. Instead, he headed through the woods on the trail that lead back towards the beach. He barked, and sniffed, then suddenly sat down. He looked up at her as he whimpered, then pawed at leaves on the trail.

"What is it, buddy?" She ran her hand back over the top of his head to calm him down. "What, someone was here, hmm? Was it Mary?" She swept her gaze around the area. She didn't see anything, but trees, plants and leaves. Pilot dug into the leaves again. She caught sight of something, it looked plastic. When she grabbed it and pulled it out from under the leaves, she discovered it was a plastic keyring. She turned it over and found that there was a photograph inside. It was a faded photo of a man holding a baby. Her heart skipped a beat. The photo was old. As she looked closer at the photo she realized that the man in the photo looked a bit like Bert. She got the distinct impression that this picture was linked to the murder and who took Mary. She opened the keyring and removed the picture. She flipped the picture over to see if there was anything written on the back of the photograph. There was a drawing of the outline of a bird. She looked up from the photograph to Pilot and studied his deep brown gaze. What did he know that she didn't?

"Suzie!" Paul's voice cut through her thoughts.

"Let's go, Pilot." She called him to her as she headed out of the woods and back down the beach towards the house. Paul ran towards her, his cheeks flushed, and his eyes filled with concern.

"Don't do that! Don't ever do that!"

"What?" She gasped as she saw the fear in his eyes.

"I looked down the beach and I couldn't see you. I didn't know you were going back into the woods. I thought you were gone!" He caught his breath, then rested his hands on her shoulders. "Please, don't scare me like that."

"I'm sorry." She frowned as she held out the photograph and keyring in her hand. "Pilot found this." She paused as she wrapped her arms around him. "I'm sorry, I didn't mean to frighten you."

He kissed her cheek, then the top of her head, and held her so tight that she squirmed a bit.

"It's okay, you're safe, that's all that matters. What's this?" He gazed at the picture.

"I think it's a clue. I think the man in this photo might be Bert."

"I agree." Paul looked at the photo closely. "Kai also mentioned that Bert was going into the woods tonight."

"He's our best lead. We need to try to find him. We need to speak to the others. Whoever we can. Someone has to know something."

"Let's do that." He wrapped his arm around her shoulders and led her away from the woods.

～

*a*s the blindfold was whipped off over Mary's head, a wave of dizziness rushed over her. It took her a few blinks before she could focus on her surroundings. She was surrounded by stone, but the floor was wood. As she attempted to pinpoint exactly where she was, images of different places flicked through her mind. None seemed exactly right. The man who captured her, stepped in front of her, and for the first time she had her suspicions confirmed.

Bert stood before her. Someone she had presumed was a harmless bird enthusiast was now a murderer and her captor. Her heart sank as she realized he didn't hesitate to let her see who he was. Which she believed meant he had no intention of leaving her alive.

"Bert? What's going on? How could you do this to me?" She did her best to sound more confused than frightened.

"Don't bother, all right?" He stared at her. "I know that you were in my room. I saw you through the window going through my stuff. I know that you've been lurking around, listening in on conversations. I know that you worked out my secret and believe I killed Ken. I don't think there's any point to dancing around the truth. Do you?"

"I was just replenishing your towels. I forgot to do it this morning. Please, you're confused, Bert. All of this was just a mistake."

"A mistake?" He chuckled. "Is that what you're going with? Do you really think I'm going to fall for that?" He crouched down in front of her and looked into her eyes. "Mary, I know what you found in my room. It was my foolish mistake to leave it there. I didn't think anyone would go into my room. I guess you put two and two together, didn't you?"

She remained silent. She knew anything that she said would only make her situation worse.

"Okay, if you want to play ignorant, I'll just spell it out for you. Callie is my daughter. I left her and her mother when Callie was only three weeks old." He shook his head.

"Why don't you refer to her as your daughter?"

"Oh, you see Callie doesn't know that I'm her father, yet. I hadn't seen her since she was a baby and only caught up with her recently."

"How did you catch up with Callie after all these years?"

"That was pure luck." He smiled. "It was pure coincidence that we met at a local birding excursion together. Callie got her love for birds from her mother. That is how I met her mother, in a bird-watching group."

"Why haven't you told her who you are?" Mary was intrigued, but also wanted to keep him talking. It might delay him from doing what he had planned.

"When I tell her the truth I wanted to make a grand gesture, by providing her with a Little Furn, her favorite bird."

"Then why did you kill Ken?"

"Well, that was just unfortunate timing. While I was climbing the tree to retrieve one of the eggs from the nest, Ken caught me. He laughed at me. He called me a hypocrite. He said I accused him of damaging the environment and look at what I was doing now. I mean how dare he? I'm nothing like him."

"What happened?" Mary asked.

"I just lost it. I knocked him out and then I couldn't stop myself." He sighed as he stood up again. "I know, I know. It seems like I'm a terrible person. But I couldn't stand him. It was like he was making fun of me. Who knows what he would say about me with that big mouth of his, and not only would I never be able to work in birding again, Callie might hate me. My plan was to hatch the egg, and give her the baby bird when it was strong enough. I still have to get the egg. After I killed Ken I heard people in the woods so I couldn't risk going back up the tree. If only the police had opened the trail sooner, I might have had the egg by now and my group would have been long gone."

"All of this over a bird?" The words spilled out of Mary's mouth. "I guess, more accurately, it's over a girl. Hmm?"

"Not just any bird. Callie's favorite bird. I had hoped she would see that I am sorry and forgive me. I made a mistake when she was born, but it's different now. I tried to see Callie when she was older, but her mother never let me see her again after I had left. She kept me from my daughter and now Callie doesn't even know who I am." His voice raised with every word he spoke as if he might become enraged. Then, as suddenly as the anger came, it dispersed, and he turned towards the lone window in the structure. "It's beautiful here, isn't it?" He gazed out through the window. "I can see why you like to live here."

"It's brought me so much peace." She watched him closely. Despite his relaxed tone, she could tell that his muscles were tense, and his body was poised to attack. "Please, Bert, just let me go. I'm not going to cause you any trouble."

"I can't do that, Mary, you know I can't." He slowly turned back to face her. Framed by the moonlight through the window, for an instant he looked harmless. Then she saw the glint in his eye, as hard and cold as a diamond. "I didn't expect either of us to be in this position, but here we are."

"We don't have to be here. We can come up with a solution for this if we work together." She shifted in her chair, which reminded her that her hands and feet were tied to the chair.

"There is only one solution here. I can't leave behind someone who knows the truth. Kai has to go down for his father's death. It's the only solution. As long as there is someone to blame for Ken's death, I will get away with it, no one will look in my direction. So, as you can see, you're too much of a risk for me. The only reason you're still alive is because I haven't figured out what I'm going to do with you. Beloved Mary, you won't disappear easily, will you?" He laughed as he turned back to the window. "Ken, he was no great loss. I'm sure there are more than a few people who are relieved by his death. But your death, it will be a local tragedy, and then of course there are the children you leave behind." He glanced back at her. "Sons, daughters?" He shook his head. "It doesn't matter. There is no way to fight fate, and your destiny is now set in stone. But I can't have anyone getting suspicious about another dead body in this beautiful town. So, you're going to have to have an unfortunate accident." He rubbed his hands together as he studied her. "I just have to figure out what it's going to be."

Mary gritted her teeth in an attempt to hide her fear. She had no doubt anymore. Bert was a killer, and she was going to be his next victim.

CHAPTER 16

As soon as Suzie saw Sebastian she knew that he was hiding something. His cheeks were flushed, and his eyes danced nervously around the dining room.

"Sebastian!" She walked straight towards him. "Tell me where Bert is."

"I don't know." He frowned.

"Don't lie to me! Mary is missing, and if you had anything to do with it —"

"Of course he didn't." Tammy stepped between them. "Suzie, why would you think that?"

"I think Bert is the one who took her, and I think Sebastian knows where."

"Bert wouldn't do that, he wouldn't hurt Mary. He's not a bad person." Tammy turned to her husband. "Tell her the truth, Sebastian, tell her who Bert really is."

"No! You know we're not supposed to share that information." Sebastian glared at her.

"That's it!" Wes suddenly shoved Sebastian back against the wall of the dining room. "You're going to tell me exactly what you know before I count to five. Got it?"

Suzie winced with fear. She'd seen the way that Sebastian could fight. Wes didn't stand a chance.

Luckily, Sebastian didn't fight back, instead, he seemed to get very calm.

"I don't know if he took her. He's my teacher, all right? My master." He looked at Wes. "I've been his student for over five years."

"Are you saying he's a skilled martial artist?" Suzie's breath grew short. That would explain quite a few things.

"Yes, he's taught me everything I know. But I am supposed to keep our training secret, he never wanted it to be public knowledge. But while we've been here, I have trained with him a few times. He always wanted to do it in private. He found a spot we could do that."

"Where?" Suzie pressed.

"Near the docks. An old, empty building. I think it might have been a boathouse at one point."

"I know where that is. Let's go." Paul grabbed Suzie's hand, then looked back at Sebastian. "You'd better hope we find her unharmed. Did you know he killed Ken?"

"No, I suspected it, though." Sebastian shuddered. "But, I didn't think he would ever hurt Mary. I really didn't."

"We don't have time for this." Wes guided Suzie and Paul out through the front door.

Paul drove straight towards the docks, but veered left before he reached them.

"There used to be another set of docks over here, but it's all grown over now." He navigated down the thin road to the end. "This must be it!" Paul pointed to the small building, a boathouse that looked like it hadn't been used in years.

"She's in there, I know it!" Suzie exclaimed.

As soon as Paul pulled the car off to the side of the road, Suzie swung the door open. Pilot jumped out and took off at a full gallop towards the building with Suzie behind him.

"Suzie, wait!" Paul charged after her, but she had a head start.

When Suzie spotted the camera, her heart

dropped. She was worried that whoever was inside, could see her coming. As torturous as it was for her, she veered off away from the building. She ran in a new direction and quietly called for Pilot to follow her. She was worried that Pilot was going to bark so she knelt down next to him and placed a finger to her lips. "Sh!" Pilot wagged his tail. When Paul caught up with her she grabbed him by the arm and pointed to the camera. "He's watching. He knows we're looking for her, and he's watching."

"That's why we need to have a plan. I've already called Jason, he's on his way. We should wait until he gets here. He said that Red confirmed that Bert had hired a car from him."

"Where is Wes?" She looked back towards the car. "Did you see where he went?"

"No, I didn't, I was busy chasing after you." He frowned. "Just take a breath, we're going to get her out of there, Suzie, but we have to be smart about this."

"We can't just wait here, Paul! He could be doing anything to her in there! He could be hurting her!" Just as she was about to bolt towards the boathouse again, Paul held her back. He wrapped his arms tight around her, and spoke gently into her ear.

"You can't help her this way, Suzie, we have to be smart about this. When Jason gets here he'll sort this out."

"When Jason gets here it will be too late. We have to do something!" She picked up a pebble from the sand and stared at it for a moment, then she flung it hard against the roof of the boathouse. The pebble thumped off the aluminum. "Maybe we can distract him enough to draw him outside. If we can get him away from Mary, then I could go in there to get her." She turned back to Paul, prepared to face his disagreement.

"It's worth a shot!" He reached down and grabbed a handful of sand, as well as pebbles, then flung them hard at the roof.

Suzie joined in with the barrage. They remained out of sight of the camera, but the available cover was sparse. She knew the moment that he stepped outside, he would spot them, and the element of surprise would be gone. He would react, and she had no idea what that reaction would be. Now that she knew he was highly trained, she was certain he didn't even need a weapon to cause Mary harm. What if he had already harmed her? She grabbed another handful of pebbles and threw hard at the roof of the boathouse. As the pebbles showered down she fought back tears. No matter what she had to do, she would save Mary.

~

$\mathcal{M}$ary shuddered as Bert paced back and forth, from one end of the building to the other. Though she'd been trying to figure out exactly where she was, she still didn't have any idea. It was unnerving to not be able to place where she was in the world. She knew she had to be close to home. She could smell salt in the air, and in the distance she thought she heard the rush of the waves. But that didn't narrow much down for her. She didn't know the area as well as Suzie did. Her thoughts shifted to her friend. Her heart broke for her as she knew that she had to be beside herself with worry. If only she'd been more careful, maybe she could have prevented this from happening. But as she stood right beside her best friend in the woods, she hadn't heard a single twig, or a leaf rustle.

One of his hands was over her mouth and the other was around her waist. She didn't even have the chance to fight back as he pulled her through the woods. She wasn't a small woman, she had extra weight on her body, but he'd carried her as if she was nothing. The next thing she knew she was in a car, and then she must have blacked out at some point. When he pulled her out of the trunk, he wasn't exactly gentle, and she woke up. Now, she knew that he was preparing for the worst. In the distance, she could hear sirens. She had no idea if that meant she was about to be rescued, or if they were headed in the completely opposite direction. But Bert heard them, too. He froze, then looked over at her.

"Don't worry, they're not coming here. No one knows we're here." He walked back towards her. "But I can't put this off much longer. I know it's unfair of me to let you suffer, to make you wonder when it's all going to end. That's cruel." He stepped around behind her. "There are some cliffs nearby. You must have run off, looking for the killer, and when you did, you slipped on one of the cliffs. They'll find your body at the bottom. What a terrible accident." He placed his hands on her shoulders.

She trembled under his touch.

"Don't do this, Bert, I know you don't want to."

"No, I don't. But, it has to be done. Don't worry, everyone will talk about how brave you were. You gave up your life in pursuit of solving a crime. Your children will have a reason to be proud." He slid his hands closer to her neck. "Just close your eyes, Mary. Can you hear the birds chirping?" He took a deep breath and started to close his hands around her neck. Just then a shower of thumps hit the roof, and made him jump back. "What was that?" He snarled.

Several more strikes hit the roof. Mary wriggled in the chair. She knew she only had one chance to get free.

"Someone's out there," Bert whispered as he walked towards the door. He checked a small monitor near the door, then peered out through the window. "I don't know where they are, but they're out there. Don't get any ideas in your head, Mary, they're not going to save you." He looked over his shoulder at her. "I'll handle this, and then I'll be back to deal with you."

As he stepped through the door, he pulled a gun out of his waistband.

Mary gasped. She hadn't even seen it there before. What if it was Suzie outside? Would she know that he was armed? She rocked so hard in the chair that she managed to topple it over. But it did no good, as her hands and feet were still bound around the chair. She heard footsteps, and tears formed in her eyes. He was already back to finish the job. Strong hands grasped her by the shoulders, and righted the chair. She kept her eyes closed to hide her tears.

"Don't do this, Bert."

"It's okay, Mary." Wes' voice flowed like honey through her senses. At first, she thought she might be in shock, or hallucinating, but the feel of his blade was cool against her skin as he sliced the ropes. "You're safe now, sweetheart, you're safe." He pulled her close, but pushed her almost instantly towards the door. "We have to move quickly, he's going to come back."

"Wes, he has a gun. Who else is out there?"

"Suzie, and Paul." He pulled his own weapon. "Don't worry, I'm going to take care of this. The car is straight ahead through that door. If I tell you to, you have to run straight for the car, understand?" He looked into her eyes. "Promise me."

"But—"

"Mary." He held her gaze. "Promise me you'll stay behind me and if I tell you to, you will run straight for the car, no matter what. I can't lose you. Please."

"Yes, I promise, Wes, I will." She touched his cheek, just before he thrust her behind him.

When he pushed out through the door, there was an explosion of gunfire.

"Run, Mary!" Wes demanded.

True to her word, Mary ran for the car. She wanted so badly to look back, but she was determined to keep her promise. When she heard a bark, and a scream, she could barely keep herself from looking. She'd made it to the car when she turned back, and saw Bert on the ground. Pilot had his mouth around the wrist that held the gun, and he wasn't letting go.

"Get him off me!" Bert shouted.

Wes ran forward and grabbed the gun from Bert's hand, just as Jason's patrol car squealed up to the boathouse. He jumped out with his weapon drawn.

"Suzie?" Mary searched the area for any sign of her. "Suzie, where are you?"

"I'm here." Suzie stepped out from behind the boathouse, then ran towards her, with Paul on her heels. "Mary!" She flung her arms around her friend. "Did he hurt you? Are you okay?" She cupped her cheeks and looked into her eyes.

"I'm okay." She blinked back tears. "I almost

wasn't. But something distracted him. Something that hit the roof."

"Oh, Mary, I'm so glad you're safe." Suzie hugged her again. "I love you, you know."

"I love you, too." She clung to her tightly, then glanced back at Bert. Pilot still hadn't let go of his wrist. "Pilot! Come here, pups!"

The dog growled once more, then finally let Jason take custody of Bert. As he handcuffed the man he began to read him his rights. Pilot ran towards Suzie and Mary.

As Mary basked in the warmth of her friends around her, and Pilot licked her fingertips, she realized just how lucky she was.

"If it wasn't for all of you, I'd be gone." She looked between their faces, and stroked the fur on Pilot's head. "Please, can we go home now?"

"Yes, we can." Suzie wound her arm through Mary's. "Let's go home."

The End

ALSO BY CINDY BELL

BEKKI THE BEAUTICIAN COZY MYSTERIES

Hairspray and Homicide

A Dyed Blonde and a Dead Body

Mascara and Murder

Pageant and Poison

Conditioner and a Corpse

Mistletoe, Makeup and Murder

Hairpin, Hair Dryer and Homicide

Blush, a Bride and a Body

Shampoo and a Stiff

Cosmetics, a Cruise and a Killer

Lipstick, a Long Iron and Lifeless

Camping, Concealer and Criminals

Treated and Dyed

A Wrinkle-Free Murder

SAGE GARDENS COZY MYSTERIES

Birthdays Can Be Deadly

Money Can Be Deadly

Trust Can Be Deadly

Ties Can Be Deadly

Rocks Can Be Deadly

Jewelry Can Be Deadly

Numbers Can Be Deadly

Memories Can Be Deadly

Paintings Can Be Deadly

Snow Can Be Deadly

Tea Can Be Deadly

A MACARON PATISSERIE COZY MYSTERY SERIES

Sifting for Suspects

Recipes and Revenge

Mansions, Macarons and Murder

NUTS ABOUT NUTS COZY MYSTERIES

A Tough Case to Crack

A Seed of Doubt

Roasted Penuts and Peril

HEAVENLY HIGHLAND INN COZY MYSTERIES

Murdering the Roses

Dead in the Daisies

Killing the Carnations

Drowning the Daffodils

Suffocating the Sunflowers

Books, Bullets and Blooms

A Deadly Serious Gardening Contest

A Bridal Bouquet and a Body

Digging for Dirt

CHOCOLATE CENTERED COZY MYSTERIES

The Sweet Smell of Murder

A Deadly Delicious Delivery

A Bitter Sweet Murder

A Treacherous Tasty Trail

Luscious Pastry at a Lethal Party

Trouble and Treats

Fudge Films and Felonies

Custom-Made Murder

Skydiving, Soufflés and Sabotage

WENDY THE WEDDING PLANNER COZY
MYSTERIES

ABOUT THE AUTHOR

Cindy Bell is the author of the cozy mystery series Donut Truck, Dune House, Sage Gardens, Chocolate Centered, Macaron Patisserie, Nuts about Nuts, Bekki the Beautician, Heavenly Highland Inn and Wendy the Wedding Planner.

Cindy has always loved reading, but it is only recently that she has discovered her passion for writing romantic cozy mysteries. She loves walking along the beach thinking of the next adventure her characters can embark on.

You can sign up for her newsletter so you are notified of her latest releases at http://www.cindybellbooks.com.

Made in the USA
Coppell, TX
15 November 2023

24291661R00125